The

Darkest

Hour

John Righten

Chris, Congratulations on
winning the competition
[signature]

Dedicated to my mother, Biddy, who taught me how to fight by using my brain.

My thanks to Jules, Kate and Jacky for once again translating my book into the Queen's English.

For reviews and comments on the Rogues Trilogy: *Churchill's Rogue*, *The Gathering Storm* and *The Darkest Hour*, and on *The Benevolence of Rogues*, go to

www.benevolenceofrogues.co.uk

facebook.com/theroguestrilogy

ISBN-10:1517364515
ISBN-13:978-1517364519

'The German dictator, instead of snatching the victuals from the table, has been content to have them served to him course by course ... Do not suppose that this is the end. This is only the beginning of the reckoning.'

Sir Winston Churchill

House of Commons speech following the signing of the Munich Agreement, 5 Oct 1938

Chapter 1: Shadows

September 1939, London

The little boy stumbled as he ran down the dark passage. As he threw his hands out to save himself, his spectacles flew off the end of his nose. He searched desperately for his glasses but his sight was so poor that the red haze of dawn was of little help. The boy heard the familiar footsteps behind him and, terrified, he turned to look up at the blurred figure. He caught sight of the shadow of a raised arm, which once again held a stick. The boy lifted his arm, already marked and bruised, to protect his face but saw another shadowy arm reach up and grab the weapon that was about to fall on him.

February 1939, Paris

'Uncouth Irish ruffian, please sit and have tea with me.'

Sean was surprised at the welcome, it politely than most he had heard recently. At least he was not referred to as The Englander. The man continued, 'You are a friend of Lenka?'

'She would be the first to disagree with you, but let's say we work together.'

'Then let us agree that you are one of those in her extensive network that includes the great and the good.'

'I'm neither great nor good, but her contacts are certainly diverse. Last month, I discovered she is good friends with a priest here in Paris. Today she tells me to go to the Mosque on the Left Bank to meet Si Kaddour Benghabrit, the Rector of the Grand Mosque of Paris.' Sean was going to mention that Lenka also seemed to know half the prostitutes in the Rue St Denis, but he thought best not to mention this in the presence of a man of God, particularly as he needed his help. Sean smiled, as he imagined what the Rector would have made of Jocky.

The large man in his mid-fifties, wearing the traditional gown, the *thawb*, and headdress, the *keffiyeh,* replied, 'Lenka has written many letters to me over the years. She is indeed a remarkable woman.'

'What does she write to you about?'

'The first time she wrote was some ten years ago, having taken in a number of Muslim children at her orphanage in Poland. She asked for my advice on how to continue their religious teaching. Also what they should eat and if I had any spare books, including copies of the Koran, so she could help them understand the teachings of Islam.' Sean, despite his natural suspicion, cynicism and atheism, liked the man. The Rector was at ease with himself and the world, as he sat in the sunshine in the splendour of the temple forecourt. 'Lenka also has a craving to learn; she has grasped the rudiments of many languages. In her correspondence, she quotes Arabic.'

'Lenka is full of surprises, though they are not always welcome.'

'Then we are equally surprised. You can imagine mine when I received her note yesterday, informing me that I would receive a visit from "an uncouth Irish ruffian".'

'She always deliberately undersells me, so when people meet me they are delighted to discover that I am a man of culture and refinement . . . and modest about it.'

'Clearly', replied the rector, releasing an unrestrained laugh. He waved his assistant over to refill their cups with more tea. The young man walked unsteadily towards them. His movement brought Sean back to thoughts of Ursula.

'Please, describe Lenka to me, for we have never met, and she never writes about herself. All I know is that she is a young, Jewish, Polish woman.' The Rector splayed his arm out, directing the Irishman to take some honey cake from the dish beside the silver teapot.

'Tall and decidedly fat for her age', replied the Irishman, ignoring the offerings on the marble-topped table.

'A man of my age knows a lie when he is being fed one. However, I believe you construct a false image to protect her. Admirable, as these are dangerous times.' Once again, the most powerful Arab leader in France released a chuckle that animated his face in an almost childlike way. It reminded the Irishman of the English Statesman's loquacious good humour.

'Lenka believes you can help us.'

'If it does not offend Allah's teachings, then I will try. What do you require?'

'In a few days, I and some friends will return to Paris with, we hope, a number of children. Some of them may have severe disabilities, and we need to hide them until we can secure their safe passage to England.'

'Where are they now?' Sean did not reply.

'Irishman, if I am to help you, I believe I should be worthy of your trust.' The Rector reclined in his chair, indicating that their conversation was at an end.

Sean again admired the Rector, for his steely resolve that justified his position of authority.

'If Lenka is a friend, is it not enough that she asks for your help?'

'For me yes, but you ask for help because of my position, and therefore I owe it to my people to know all.'

'So be it; I have no choice but to trust you.' Sean waited for the young man who was serving tea to finish his task and depart. Once the cups were full, the young man bowed his head and very slowly, as his legs were weak, made his way from the courtyard. Before the Irishman continued, the Rector spoke.

'You need not concern yourself with my assistant. He cannot speak and has not left the Mosque once since he was first brought to me over two years ago.'

'Anyone can scribble a message.'

'True, but he communicates through his drawings.'

Sean looked quizzically at the Rector, but as time was short he returned to his mission. 'Lenka believes she has reliable information that the Nazis have built a hospital on the edge of Lake Como, just on the Italian-Swiss border. A number of disabled children have been transported there for what the intercepted Nazis correspondence terms "treatment".'

'Treatment?'

'The Nazis offering "treatment" to children with debilitating illnesses; do you know the meaning of the word "oxymoron"?'

'I do, and I understand the context in this case.'

'I, and others, intend to free the children and bring them to England. Will you help us?'

'You must tell me everything. Who is the source of this information?'

'The British.'

'Ah, the British. There is not an international affair that they do not have an interest in.

'You have issues with them?

'No more than you, Irishman.'

'I ended my battles with them some time ago. Now there is a greater threat.'

'The Nazis?'

'Yes. London has intercepted communiqués relating to numerous shipments of construction materials and medical supplies to the facility. All shipments are heavily guarded by a special joint SS/Gestapo unit. As for the purpose of the hospital there are no details, apart from the occasional reference to treatment. Again, as to what that entails we know little. One list of items contains restraining harnesses, straitjackets and manacles.'

'To treat patients with severe mental illness perhaps?'

'Do you believe that?'

The Rector did not hesitate. 'We have heard of the Nazis' genetic experiments. Does it involve a major in the Gestapo – a man called Cerberus?'

The Rector watched as the Irishman leant forwards, as he expected he would.

'What do you know about him?' asked Sean.

'A few years ago a young boy showed me some drawings depicting how this man had 'experimented' on . . .' The Rector paused as he shook his head, 'No, 'mutilated' would be the better description, having been taken prisoner during the Italian-Abyssinian war.' He lifted the cup from the table. 'Since then, I have met others who had their tongues removed, some their genitals and a large number had their eyes, cut out. He has a personal fascination with eyes it seems.'

The Rector retrieved a file from a box beside his chair and passed its contents to Sean. 'These are his sketches. Thankfully, he managed to escape from a window before this man Cerberus could remove his eyes.'

Sean carefully examined the horrific drawings. One was of what looked like a lizard whose neck and limbs stretched out far beyond the sleeves and collar of a black Gestapo uniform. In its elongated fingers were a hammer and a cut-throat razor dripping with blood. Standing next to the creature, Sean recognised the large, bald-headed man holding a cleaver in his hand and what looked like testicles in the other – Grossmann.

'What happened to the boy?' asked Sean.

'I keep him close, as his trauma has left him with the mind of a child.'

The Rector placed the drawings back in the file and

returned it to the box. 'The Jews have another name for the man you know as Cerberus. In English it means The Golem: a creature that silently ferries the innocent away in darkness. My people call him Shaytan, the Devil. Though since someone shot off part of his jaw', he smiled at Sean, 'he is known by my people as Nasnas, a part-human devil with half a face.' The Rector took a sip from his cup. 'His many names are testimony that he is a creature without a redeeming feature. He is pure evil: a sadist who tortures his victims until their hearts are about to burst. Only then does he reluctantly hand them over to his companion – who is ever present – death.'

'You would like to see him dead?'

'I am not a man of violence, but the man thrives on the pain of the innocent. I seek only justice for those he has murdered and those . . .' the Rector looked over solemnly at the young man who was now feeding crumbs to some sparrows, 'to whom he has denied a future.' The Rector paused, and then smiled at the Irishman. 'I sense you do not fear him. Indeed I believe you are eager to meet him again. But, I pray that his companion does not touch you with his skeletal finger first.'

Sean remained impassive.

The Rector continued, 'I believe it was he who led the torture of Lenka. She is gravely ill still'

Sean nodded. 'But how do you know that?'

'Her note. In places the nib had broken the parchment, her normal fluid style was replaced by clipped sentences and the ink was smudged from the moisture from her fingers. Her pain sadly, is obvious.'

'She suffered severe internal as well as external injuries.

Though the bleeding has stopped, her fever refuses to break.'

'Is she receiving proper medical care?'

'Yes, from a friend of hers, a doctor.'

'Bring her here. We have women whose medical knowledge is far superior to that practised in the Western world.'

'She refused to come here, for fear of giving away her connection with you and jeopardising the safety of you, your people and the children.' The Rector was about to protest. 'When Lenka sets her mind to something, there is no changing it.'

'So that is why you came here wearing the guise of the *thawb*, and the *keffiyeh*.'

Sean tugged on his headdress.

'Perhaps next time you will have prepared in advance and nurture some form of facial growth.' His smile disappeared. 'Where is Lenka?'

'In the depths of the Catacombs', replied Sean, without any hesitation, knowing that he had to be honest with the man to gain his cooperation.

'You have left her in that damp, rat infested crypt? Then, I will have my people go there and tend her. In a few days' time – when you deliver the children here – I will arrange transit papers to England for her, along with those for the children.'

'Are your people able to smuggle Lenka here?'

'Paris is a city of many secrets. One more will not be noticed.'

Sean looked around at the garden and the beautiful white and blue tiled walls. It was the most serene place he had ever been in. He watched the Rector's assistant stumble as he led some families who had arrived for prayer through the main door. The serenity was shattered by the Rector. 'Cerberus broke both his legs with a hammer, castrated him and, only once his screams were exhausted, did he cut his tongue out.'

The Irishman continued to watch the young man who was offering an array of sweetmeats to the children from a tray. 'You will help us?'

'Yes', came the voice of the Rector.

Sean turned to the man. 'I once posed a similar question to another man. Why would you help a woman you have never met, knowing that it could bring the wrath of the authorities on you?'

'Lenka has only ever asked for my help to assist my people.'

Sean expected that the man knew who was involved, but felt he had to be explicit. 'The children, as I'm sure you have gathered, will most likely be Jewish.'

'There is a quote from the scriptures known to both Arab and Jew, "Save one life, and it is as if you have saved all of humanity". Arab, Jew or gentile, children are children. I pray the day never comes when we forget that.'

'We will only know how many children there will be once we are inside the hospital; there may be adults too. It will then take time for your people to create their papers. In the meantime, if we bring the children to Paris, can you hide them?'

'Arab and Jew share many customs. Neither eats pork, our male children are circumcised and to an unfamiliar ear even our names are similar. We certainly have more in common than we do with our Christian hosts, the French. Gentiles, particularly the thugs in jackboots, are in the main ignorant of any religion, so there is little risk of them or their network of informers detecting the nuances that separate our beliefs. That is why I believe I can help the Jewish children without risking the lives of my people. I will deal with any random visitations by the French authorities', he said as he opened his hands wide and looked around the courtyard. 'The children are welcome here.'

The Irishman thanked the man as he rose from the table.

The Rector bid him goodbye by bringing his hands together and bowing his head. He looked at Sean and smiled. 'The scar is deep in your cheekbone. Is that when you were involved in the bloody incident that the newspapers described, very melodramatically, as The Battle of London some months ago?'

Sean said nothing now that the Rector had agreed to help and though he liked the man, he felt no reason to tell him more than he had to.

'Like your nemesis, you have many names. The Nazis call you The Englander.'

Sean remained impassive.

'You are also called by your enemies the Jew lover.' Sean said nothing. 'It is said that when one has the blue eyes of The Englander fixed upon them, the next pair of eyes they see are those of the Devil.' The Rector smiled. 'Yet I see this is a fallacy, for your eyes are grey and partly green. I am pleased to see that you are indifferent to your notoriety. Many men, whose lives are surrounded by death, come to believe they are indestructible and become consumed by their own self-importance.' Again Sean said nothing. 'They should add the Muslim lover to their list, for your interventions saved a number of our women and children during the war in Ethiopia.'

'Children have no say in the religion they are born into yet there are those who would kill them for it.'

'If we never meet again, I thank you on behalf of my people that you saved. One other thing Eng–'

'Irishman.'

The Rector smiled. 'Irishman – speaking of eyes, you are in the eye of the storm. If you stray beyond it, I ask that you do not take Lenka with you.'

'In her condition, Lenka is going nowhere for a while.'

'Then Allah be with you. Cerberus will be waiting for you, and he has created a legion of psychopaths to guard him.'

Sean nodded his head, as he set off to walk past the sparrows bathing in the blue fountain in the centre of the courtyard. As Sean adjusted the *keffiyeh* on his head, he looked across at the Rector's assistant. The young man sat cross-legged on the floor playing counting games with the children – but he was unable to join in with their laughter.

Chapter 2: The Battle of London

November 1938, London

Sean Ryan opened his eyes. 'Not another fucking hospital!'

He felt the usual pains tearing at him: the torn muscles in his right shoulder that hated to be disturbed and the pins holding his right leg together that angrily made their presence known. But, to his surprise, the only other pain was when he lifted his head to find the blood that had oozed through his stitches in the back of his head had dried to the pillow.

'What's the damage?' he asked the nurse changing the gauze on his cheek.

'A very nasty cut to the back of your head and an inch-long slice out of your cheek.'

'What, no bullets to extract? Bloody hell, this is the best shape I've been in years.'

Unimpressed, the nurse continued. 'There are some men outside to see you.'

'If they're wearing dog-collars and are here to give me my last rites tell them to bugger off and come back later.'

The nurse smiled this time and as she left said, 'By the looks of your visitors you may not be long for this world.'

'Don't get up Ryan,' said the first of the two men strode into the room, brushing passed the nurse as she left.

'I had no intention of doing so,' now that Sean gleaned

from their polished cheeks they were public school, while their buttoned, tan coloured trench coats confirmed they were secret service.

'Why did members of the criminal underworld try to kill you?'

'The underworld,' said Sean, making no attempt to hide his disdain. 'Remind me: What does the Intelligence bit mean in British Intelligence?'

'The other cars that you destroyed were found to have stolen boxes of cigarettes and crates of brandy in the boot. We have also heard that there is a contract out on you to the value of–'

'I'm not interested.'

'So back to my question, why is the under–'

'Any identification found on the bodies?' said Sean.

'Considering there were nine corpses, either burnt or full of bullets, there were unsurprisingly few personal items found intact on them.'

'Not that surprising,' said Sean.

The Irishman knew that once again, Cerberus had covered his tracks well enough to fool those who would not look too deeply. The supposedly illegal contraband also explained why the cars blew up so easily – it also highlighting their overconfidence in carrying such an flammable cargo on such a mission.

'Were you the one who surprised my assailant?' asked Sean of the elder man in his mid-twenties with wiry ginger hair.

'Yes, but back to my–'

'Did you see his face?'

'No, he escaped in a gun-metal grey Duesenberg.'

'Thanks for answering my questions. Now fuck off, unless you're arresting me.'

'Lieutenant Brett has confirmed that it was the two of you who were attacked. As a result of her statement, my superiors have decided to release you. But, first I have a few questions for–'

'The lieutenant is alive?'

'She is very lucky to be alive and is in this hospital, but now for my–'

'As I said, fuck off.'

The other man, barely out of his teens, tall, with a pinched face, drew his revolver as spoke. 'Paddy, you better show due respect to His Majesty's–'

'By the time you pull back the trigger, the barrel will be jammed up your arse.'

The two British agents exchanged embarrassed glances, shrugged and left the room.

The Irishman got dressed and found a very welcome gift hidden under his battered leather jacket, a weathered Mauser automatic pistol. Once he eased himself into his clothes, he set off down the corridor. He leafed through the register at the vacant reception desk, found what he was looking for and headed off to the women's private wing.

Sean entered to find Lieutenant Brett asleep. Her face was paler than he thought possible, no doubt due to the wound beneath the large cotton pad taped to her neck. The Irishman looked at her clothes which were draped over a chair. Even from a distance he could see the black powder marks on the blood-stained white cotton blouse that surrounded two bullet holes. The first was in the left-hand side and the second had partially removed a section of the collar on the same side. He walked over to the woman's bed and gently lifted the cotton pad and gauze that lay over the half-inch bullet hole just in the side of her neck. Sean surmised from the hole that there must be an exit wound on the other side, for at that range the bullet would have gone straight through.

'Satisfied now? Is that all you came for?' said the woman, as her eyes opened.

'Look, I need to know–'

'Need! You're only here because you need information, you don't give a damn that I was nearly killed. I'll tell you what you need to know – that Polish bitch of yours was behind all this. Don't bother asking anything of me until you have killed her. Get out!'

Amelia looked away as she lifted her shawl to cover her neck. Sean heard her say softly, 'She betrayed us.'

Sean said nothing, but before he closed the door behind him he heard her start to weep.

Two hours later Ryan walked past a gun-metal grey supercharged Duesenberg SJ Riviera Phaeton and entered Blades, the illustrious gentlemen's club. He did so not through the main door, but through a window leading into the kitchen at the rear of the building. A few minutes later, after finding the name of the person he was looking for under one of the bells that summoned the servants from the kitchen, he entered a room on the top floor. Once inside, Ryan pointed the Mauser at Colonel Sebastian Penhaligon; a member of British Intelligence and thanks to the Irishman one of the few surviving members of the Cairo Gang.

'Hello, Paddy,' said the colonel, as he looked towards the drawer of his mahogany desk. The colonel knew it was futile to attempt to make a grab for the revolver inside it – but he didn't need to.

Ryan looked over at the man who had shielded himself behind a pregnant chambermaid in a Dublin hotel room sixteen years earlier.

'You were expecting me?' asked Ryan.

'You are easier to read than my daughter's nursery books. Having survived, I knew you would seek me out. You recognised me, but I knew you wouldn't tell anyone as you are the type that is a lone wolf and will trust no one but yourself. However, I am surprised you found me so quickly.'

'English gentlemen are more at home at their club than they are with their family.'

'I have a room here, as does my daughter. The Club has adopted her, but God knows why. We are at opposite ends of the same wing – you would understand why if you ever saw the wretched creature.'

'That's the second time you've mentioned your daughter, you must be hoping that because you have family I will spare your life.'

The colonel smiled, 'It was worth a try Paddy.'

'Before I blow your brains over the tiger hide on the wall behind you, tell me why didn't you kill me two days ago?'

'My orders were to kill you, but we were disturbed. The British agents sent to protect Lieutenant Brett appeared and started shooting, but I managed to escape.'

'Bollocks, you had me at point blank range and you

don't strike me as someone who is easily startled.'

'Very astute. Sadly, I am at the mercy of my indulgences. I used the intervention of British Intelligence as an excuse to let you live.'

'Kindness is a virtue, and you don't have any.'

'When you and your rag-tail assassins wiped out my colleagues in the Cairo Gang in Dublin, it stymied my career. We have unfinished business, and I want your death to be an extraordinarily painful one.'

'You sound like your boss, Cerberus.'

'The only man I would ever fear to cross. But the opportunity to exact my revenge in the manner of my choosing was simply too much to resist. I take it your interest in knowing more about my commander is the reason that I too am still alive?'

Ryan said nothing as he scanned the room in search of a diary and an address book.

'Admiring my arsenal of weapons?' asked Penhaligon.

Ryan had noticed that there were few books in the room, and those on display could be only partially seen as they were masked by an array of swords, daggers and throwing knives. There were perhaps two hundred hand weapons nesting on shelves or secured to the walnut-panelled walls.

'Psychology is not my field,' said Ryan, 'but Freud would conclude that all of this is compensating for an exceptionally small dick.'

'One day you Paddies will finally be taught to respect your betters.'

A side door opened behind the desk.

Penhaligon spun around and swept up a little girl, six

or perhaps seven years old, locking her neck with his arm. The German manufactured Steffi teddy bear in her arms landed silently on the carpet. He turned to face Ryan, this time smiling, as he positioned her directly between himself and the gun. 'This is my cretin of a daughter.' He lifted her up higher to cover his face. 'She is simple, as they politely call it, but after all these years of being embarrassed by her existence I have finally found a use for her.'

'Again, you use the innocent as a shield, only this time it's your own daughter.'

'Needs must and anyway she is an embarrassment to me. Sadly, we are not as advanced in the treatment of abnormalities in the species as in Germany.'

The young girl did not appear to notice the threat to her life.

'Drop the gun, and turn and face the wall. One twist of my arm and I will break her neck,' shouted Penhaligon. Ryan kept his Mauser pointed at the major's right eye which was peeking out from behind his daughter's mousey brown curls. 'Do it, or would you condemn the girl to death simply because of who her father is?'

Ryan edged to his right to get a clearer shot at the man.

'I have fought in Africa and the Middle East, but it was the Irish that were impossible to shut up. I believe it's because of your Catholic faith. You are all so sexually repressed that you keep fighting as the Church will not allow you to screw.' As he spoke, Penhaligon edged himself to his right, to ensure that his daughter covered most of his upper body and face.

Penhaligon rested his free hand on the iron figurine of

an eagle, its wings spread wide, on his desk. 'But, it's your incessant opinions of us English that we find the most irritating.'

Ryan curled his figure around the trigger, waiting for the man to throw the iron statue at him.

A violent surge of electricity seized Ryan's body, throwing him backwards across the room. He landed on the floor against a bookcase. As he turned, a knife swished through the air and embedded itself in the bookcase an inch from his left ear.

Penhaligon had now reached the drawer of the desk. He grabbed the revolver. But Ryan rolled four times across the floor towards the Mauser. He grabbed it and fired a shot into the pot of wooden quills on the desk, sending the metal points of two of them up into the air until they came to a stop in Penhaligon's face and neck. The recoil sent spears of pain through the Irishman's right shoulder. The man screamed as he stood up from the desk, as Ryan's second shot removed most of the man's gun hand, along with the revolver, sending them across the desk. A third bullet disappeared into the upper left corner of the British officer's forehead.

Despite his injuries, Penhaligon managed to rip a twelfth-century broadsword from the wall and leapt over the desk. As he did so, he tipped the iron eagle on his desk to one side. It released a second large electric charge through the cables running under the carpet to the iron rods that secured the shelves to the walls. Ryan was up on one knee as the charge threw him forward across the room. The rubber mat positioned under the desk once again isolated Penhaligon, and his daughter, from the shock.

Repeated blows of the sword rained down towards Ryan, just missing him, helped by the fact the British officer had only one hand to hold it.

'I see those fucking blue eyes are staring up at me once more,' screamed Penhaligon. 'But I'll close them for good this time.' The colonel continued to slash at the chair that Ryan had seized and was now holding up, though it was disintegrating under the blows.

To his right Ryan could see the girl was attempting to crawl out from under the desk. The colonel's blade just missed her as he swung it back before lunging at the Irishman once again. Ryan dived towards the girl and rolled like a circus acrobat before whisking her up in his arms. Penhaligon spun around and swiped Ryan across the side of his neck with his sword, opening up a new gash just below the ten stitches in the back of his head.

Ryan kept hold of the girl and threw her under the desk as another sweep of the two-inch thick blade swept past just in front of his face as he turned round.

Penhaligon looked like some horror creation from one of Goya's darker canvases. A huge hole gaped in the side of his head, and one of the metal-tipped quills was now lodged half-way into his neck. So much blood was shooting from his wounds that it was hard to believe that the man was alive, let alone waving a broadsword above his head. Ryan assumed an attacking stance, just as Penhaligon was about to bring down the blade and slice the Irishman in half. Ryan launched the heels of his boots into Penhaligon's chest sending him backwards into the book case. As the British officer crashed into the shelves, Ryan smashed his boot into the iron eagle perched on the desk. Penhaligon screamed, as sizzling sparks shot out of the silver fillings in his mouth, the metal nibs protruding from his face and neck and the blade he held above his head.

The British officer fell back towards the door as his daughter began to scurry towards her father. Ryan lifted his foot up and the eagle sprang upright again.

Penhaligon saw Ryan's revolver lying on the floor, less than a metre in front of his daughter. With his last breath, he screamed at his only child. 'Fucking give it to me, you cretin!'

With tears welling up in her eyes, the girl looked at her father. She ignored the gun and lifted up the rusty-coloured teddy bear beside it and placed it in her father's bloodied hand. He was about to scream something, but his face froze in fury.

Sean walked over to the girl and knelt down beside her. Through the banging on the door accompanied by the clash of something heavy being rammed into it, he spoke softly. 'Your father said that the people here are kind to you.' Looking closer, he saw that the little girl's eyes were crossed and that neither met his. 'I'm sorry, but I have to leave now.'

Again the girl did not acknowledge his words, but to Sean's surprise she lifted the teddy bear from her father's hand and pressed it against the wound to the side of his neck. 'Thank you,' said Sean. 'I will keep this, only so I can clean it and send it back to you.'

He hugged her tightly, but the girl did not respond.

'My words will mean little, but I will make sure that you are well cared for.'

Sean collected the Mauser as he raised himself up. He

guided the girl so she was behind him, before he threw the chair by the desk through the window.

The girl looked up at the Irishman with bemusement as he dived out of the shattered window frame. Then, she dropped to her knees beside her father and began to stroke his blood-soaked hair.

Chapter 3: A Message from America

March 1939, Paris

Jake looked at the grey stone building. His French was not on a par with his German, but he understood the etching on the stone plaque above the forbidding oak door:

Cimetière des Saints Innocents
Fermé 1780

The sight of the Catacombs did nothing to cheer him after his arrival in Paris a few hours earlier. That morning, the only laughter he had heard was that of children during the two hours it had taken him to walk through the back streets of the city from the Gare du Nord to the Left Bank. There was no evidence of the city's famous *joie de vivre*. Parisians either looked bewildered or subdued, whilst others could not hide their fear. Jake knew why. The newspaper headlines on the stands declared that the Nazis had marched into Czechoslovakia, but for once the paper sellers were reluctant to cry out the headlines.

The tall, blond-haired American pulled the US Marine Corps knife from inside his left sleeve. He slipped the tip through the gap in the door frame and carefully worked the bolt on the other side loose from the frame. Two minutes later, he was making his way down the stone staircase. When he reached the bottom of the 300 steps, he heard a familiar voice.

'You might as well have brought a brass band with you with those boots.'

'Take that gun out of my ear Irishman before I ram it down your throat.'

'Good to see you, Yank,' replied Sean, placing the Webley back into his leather belt.

'How's Lenka?' asked the American.

'Not good, and the news that Czechoslovakia has fallen hasn't helped.'

'How the hell does she expect to make a full recovery in this hell hole?'

'Believe me, I've tried to get her out of here, but you know Lenka and once she digs her heels in that's it.'

'Then we have more chance of getting her out of this place by lifting this mausoleum out of the ground with her in it,' replied the American. Jake spotted the reflection of small darting eyes in the eye sockets of the skulls as he passed. Shunning the light from Sean's candle, the rats scurried away from the bones mounted up on the walls.

'How many skulls are down here?' asked Jake.

'You know what, I haven't got around to counting them,' said Sean, as he turned to lead the way. As he did so, Jake noticed the wound on the side of his neck. 'Apart from that slice out of your cheek, I heard that the head wound you received in London was under your hairline.'

'It's one I picked up later. It's just me I guess, I seem to aggravate people. Lenka had some fun stitching it up though,' he laughed as he bent his head to make his way through the six-foot-high passage.

'Is that dumb Bear with her?'

'He arrived an hour ago, but something's wrong. He just clasped me by the shoulder and said it was good to see me.'

'Brain damage, it was just a matter of time.'

'I asked him if he found his family and he said nothing.'

'His wife has probably run off with the Moscow Philharmonic.'

'He didn't mention his daughter.'

Jake made no derogatory comment this time. 'Then they're dead. Jesus, Sean, the war hasn't even begun, and it feels as if each of us has already lost everything. Any news of Chris?'

The man in the increasingly battered black leather jacket walking ahead of him did not answer. Perhaps, the Irishman did not hear him as rain water continued to seep into the passage, triggering more echoes as it landed in the puddles below.

Jake followed Sean as he turned into a small dark alcove, and there was Lenka lying beneath an old blanket on a bed of wooden boxes. Vodanski wore a solemn look as he stood over her. He did not acknowledge the American.

A few lighted candles nestled in holes in the walls of the vault, like sentries guarding the stacks of bones beneath them. Though she raised a smile when she saw him, Jake was struck by the paleness of her skin, which matched that of the lumps of moist calcium on the walls.

'A reunion of dysfunctional outcasts, and where better to hold it,' said Jake, as he looked at the shadows skipping over the skulls as candle flames of the candles danced in the draught. 'The Cossack would feel at home here, the miserable bastard.'

Vodanski did not look at the American. 'Irishman, I thought I saw the Cowboy earlier, but it was a deformed skull lying amongst the rat shit.' Then he glanced over towards an indistinguishable pile in the corner.

Lenka listened to the familiar childish banter between the male Rogues. Jake and Vodanski used to quarrel when they first fought together in Madrid, but after Dominique's death neither acknowledged the presence of the other. It used to infuriate her. However, over the past four months, alone beneath the city, she would think of those times. She understood that it was a game they played to shackle their hatred of each other and stop it erupting into violence. The adolescent humour was also the way that men, especially the three around her, dealt with pain. Lenka had known many, men and women, who would never talk about loss; instead they kept it locked away deep down inside them. She knew that it was futile to go in search of it, as it would only release the rage inside them.

Jake sat on the bed as Lenka raised her arms up so that he could gently lift her up and hold her. He could feel how weak she was. She had lost a couple of stone or more; her skin was dripping with sweat, and her breath was barely noticeable on his cheek.

He kissed her on the forehead and whispered in her ear, 'Be careful of the Irishman.' She dropped her head back and nodded as if to say she understood. Jake lowered her carefully back onto the bed. Lenka's face was gaunt and her skin almost translucent, no doubt due to being underground for so long. She grimaced and though her injuries had happened some time ago, it reminded the men of how close to death she had come.

'Don't look so worried Jake. Believe me, I'm much better now. My friend Bridgette comes with food and has nursed me back to health. I'll be . . . "riding your ass" as you used to say, soon enough.'

Her blanket slipped down revealing her breasts which seemed a little bit bigger than Jake remembered.

'Come on, let us cover you,' said Jake, but Vodanski was already lifting the blanket up over her shoulders.

'Nothing you three haven't seen before,' mumbled Lenka.

The men looked at each other. Then Jake smiled at Lenka, 'Ah, fuck it, I'm still introducing you to my mother.'

Jake stood up, to let Sean take his place. The Irishman dipped the cotton towel he had in his hand into the bowl of water. For the past two days since he had returned to Paris, he had taken care of Lenka. It gave Bridgette a break, so she could spend a few uninterrupted days in her office in the Museé du Louvre. As the Catacombs fell under the French woman's jurisdiction, it meant her daily visits to the crypt to clean and provide food for Lenka had not aroused suspicion.

'We've got to get you out–' said Jake.

'As I've told these two idiots. No,' replied Lenka. 'I'm staying here until this latest fever breaks, and I can finally stand on my own two feet and I am able to fight. Until then, I'm staying here as the Gestapo has informers everywhere, even in Paris, and knowing I'm in the city, they will not rest until they have found me.'

'Okay Lenka, now that we are all here why did you summon us to Paris?' asked Sean.

'I only passed on the message. It is Jake that's brought us to Paris.'

Jake read the men's faces: he was not surprised to see their anger as they knew he now worked for the US Government. He was prepared. For the first time in nearly a year, the American acknowledged Vodanski's presence.

'I knew you wouldn't come if I asked you and–'

The Russian clenched his fists. 'You're going to join the skulls behind you.'

The Irishman added, 'I'm with the Bear for once. I am sick of being manipulated. You better have a good reason as I'm on no government's payroll.'

'I'd feel the same. Look, just give me a few moments, and I'll tell you what I know and then you can help me or fuck off. I've also brought a friend.'

Vodanski and Sean placed their hands on their revolvers.

'Don't worry. It's not a trap. He only has one leg, so he wouldn't get down here until Christmas.'

'Samuel!' said the astonished Sean. Jake nodded, while Vodanski briefly seemed to smile at the news. 'You brought him to France, why?'

'When I returned home I went in search of him to make sure he was OK. Over a drink, I told him what I was up to. The next thing is he says he has influential friends in Paris that can help and that he was coming with me.'

'A one-legged black man with no money or an arse to his trousers,' smiled Sean. 'What choice did you have? Still, it will be good to see him again.'

Jake produced a blueprint that looked like one of those that Jocky had swiped from the factory in Amsterdam. He began to unfurl it, laying it across the blanket covering Lenka.

'Great, now I'm only of use as a table. And who the fuck is Samuel anyway?' With that, Lenka turned and wrapped her arms around Sean's waist.

The American and the Russian were equally surprised at her open embrace. 'Sometimes with you two, I feel as if I've walked in half-way through a film as I haven't a clue what is going on,' commented Jake.

The American returned to the unfurled blueprint, placing his hands firmly on the corners to hold it open. 'As you probably gathered, these are what Jocky stole. We got some of our experts to examine them. The first thing they discovered was that the comments on the drawings are not relevant to the graphics of the machinery parts.'

'What do they say?' asked Lenka.

'Our guys tell us it's to do with engineering but not mechanical engineering.'

'Civil?' said Sean.

'Social,' replied Jake.

Vodanski pointed to a script on the blueprint. 'Jocky recognised some of the chemical symbols.'

'Yes,' replied Jake. 'But, he could not have determined the compound as the percentage of each element is written in German rather than marked in figures.'

'You two have had your Eureka moment,' looking at Jake and Vodanski, 'and you're finally acting like civilised human beings, but if I wasn't already confused enough, what do you mean by social engineering?' asked Sean.

'Our experts—'

'The American military,' interrupted Vodanski.

'In Harvard,' continued Jake. 'Our scientists there believe the Nazis are trying to produce something that can alter human molecular structure, either to destroy impurities,' he looked at the other three Rogues, 'or to create mutations.'

After years of refusing to acknowledge the American's existence, Vodanski abandoned all pretence at playing games.

'Your military scientists believe the Nazis can do this?'

'No, our experts think it's all hokum.'

'What is hokum?' asked the Russian.

'It means bollocks,' replied Sean.

'It's more than bollocks,' replied Jake. 'The chemical compounds – in all cases – are lethal to the host.'

'For what propose?' asked Sean

'The State Department has intercepted messages from Berlin. We have learnt that Cerberus' Alpha Wolves are building some new facility on the edge of Lake Como, which is situated on the Italian–Swiss border. From what we have deciphered, there is some form of animal testing underway. We believe the experiments being carried out are related to these blueprints. They may even be working on the ones Jocky tampered with and left behind.'

'The Nazis don't bother with animals,' said Lenka quietly. 'Is Cerberus there?'

Jake shook his head. 'Since his encounter with you and Sean, your friend has withdrawn to Berlin. His victims are now brought to him. He has had elaborate interrogation equipment installed on his train. Our agents say he never leaves his carriage, and such is his caution that he has the train moved between various sidings within the city every night. He is protected around the clock by a squadron of his heavily armed Alpha Wolves.'

'They are there not just to protect him,' said Lenka. 'When I was being tortured he boasted that he was compiling dossiers on all those who posed a threat to the Nazis or were deemed subversive.'

'Are all these dossiers on his train?' asked Jake.

'We can only know that if we get inside it.' Lenka asked another question of Jake. 'Is Rerck with him?'

'Who is Rerck?' replied Jake.

Lenka fixed her eyes on Jake. 'Cerberus is the brains; Rerck is the brawn. From what Sean and I witnessed in Paris, Cerberus' Alpha Wolves – even the likes of psychopaths like Rerck – will not break wind unless their commander orders it. Vodanski and I have a plan. If we cut off the head of the creature, its tentacles, which stretch around the world, will fall impotent. Now that we know where Cerberus is-'

It was Sean's turn to interrupt. 'This is what Cerberus wants. So far, he has played us, and now he is baiting the trap with himself.' He lifted up the woman's pale face in his hands. 'This is still a time of peace, Lenka. I know what they have done to you, but the patients in this mysterious hospital must be our priority.'

Lenka turned her face towards the American. 'Jake?'

'For once, my personal view aligns with that of my government. I'm not about to start a war that will bring in the United States.'

Lenka looked to the Russian. 'Vodanski?'

'First the hospital. Then, I will come back, and if you are ready to fight, join me and we will head to Berlin and kill Cerberus and his Alpha Wolves.'

She lifted her pale face to look at the Russian. 'I will be ready.'

Sean turned first to Lenka and then Vodanski. 'All the battles we have fought were not just to rid the world of one psychopathic lunatic. If you launch an attack on Cerberus in the German capital, it will give the Nazis an excuse to instigate reprisals against more innocent families.'

Lenka gave Sean a look of resignation, knowing that the Irishman was right.

Vodanski was unmoved. 'You can all do what you like. I've had enough of sweeping away the prey from the beast just before it snaps its jaws shut. It is time to kill the creature.'

'You really must be a dumb bear, to dance to Cerberus' tune,' said Ryan, standing squarely in front of the Russian.

Vodanski stepped towards Ryan. 'You are a hypocrite, Irishman. You killed a Nazi informer in Berlin, less than a mile from the Reichstag.'

'You are selective with the facts, Russian. I had no choice, as the man was about to inform the SS about the children in Otto's factory.'

Vodanski's voice grew louder. 'What of other children, Irishman? As long as Cerberus is given free rein to select his next victims, more families will suffer,'

Jake slumped on the bed next to Lenka. 'These two assholes are getting carried away. First, we have the little matter of freeing a number of patients from a heavily fortified island, guarded by an elite unit of the Third Reich's deadliest killers.'

Sean ignored Jake and stepped forward towards the Russian. 'I'm in this for one reason: to save innocent families. So forget any thoughts of launching an attack on Cerberus in the heart of Berlin.'

'I will go alone,' replied Vodanski.

Sean bent his head towards Vodanski's. 'When war breaks out, I'll be ripping heads off Nazis while you're still trying to find someone to explain to you how to tie the laces on your boots.'

Jake tilted his head towards Lenka. 'There was me burying the hatchet with the dumb Russian Bear, only for a second front to open up with the Irishman.'

The Russian stepped another pace forward, placing most of his weight on his front foot. 'To stop me, you will have to put a bullet here,' he said, pressing his index finger to his forehead.

'If it means stopping you from starting World War Two, I won't give it a second thought,' replied Sean.

Lenka, looking up at Sean, asked, 'Then, will you kill me?'

Twenty minutes later the three men had climbed the stairs and emerged from the oak door as the troubled grey clouds opened. Sean made his way across Rue Froidevaux to the little park on the other side of the road. Jake and Vodanski said nothing but followed, though each had a hand on their revolvers while trying to keep them dry.

'How is she?' asked the tall man who emerged from the shadow of the building.

'Hiding her pain,' replied Sean.

Jake and Vodanski were pleased to see the big Scotsman, but their delight was tinged with sadness as it always brought back memories of the loss of Jewel.

Chris shook hands with the other two Rogues. But Sean and Vodanski began to argue once more. Chris quickly grasped the situation from the volatile exchange. He placed his hand on Vodanski's arm.

'My friend, I understand your anger and your pain. I too have no one left, but Sean is right. You will light the fuse, and even if you succeed in wiping out Cerberus and his Alpha Wolves, there will be many more to take their place. Meanwhile, the Nazis will use your actions as an excuse to mobilise. Do what you have to do. I will not stop you. I will even try to hold back Sean if you do. But understand the cost if you succeed.'

The tension in Vodanski's face disappeared. Vodanski nodded to the Scotsman. 'Lenka told me that when Jewel died, we lost our conscience. We didn't. She passed it to you.'

'Chris why didn't you join us in the Catacombs?' asked Jake.

Chris turned back to the Irishman. 'I take it you had a good reason for asking me to stay here? I trust you, Sean, but why didn't you want me to see Lenka?'

'It wasn't that I didn't want you to see Lenka,' said Sean. 'It's just we can never afford to all be in the same place at once.'

Chapter 4: Chris' Story

July 1926, Edinburgh

Chris never knew his parents or indeed anything about his family or where he came from. Even how he got to the orphanage in Edinburgh was unclear. He materialised on the orphanage's ledger as a baby boy delivered on 2 June 1914. Even this created confusion as to whether he was sent there or born in the building. The details in the comments column and the signature were illegible. Over the years, whenever he asked about his origins, the staff would only offer their profuse apologies as they were normally very proud of their meticulous record keeping. Mary, the stern and very gruff Matron, did look into it when she first arrived a few years later. 'They say the nurse who signed for you was three sheets to the wind, though in the short time I knew the lass I never smelt the drink on her breath.' His name was given to him by the Superintendent of the orphanage, Mrs Mackay, as it provided some solace after her Labrador, Chris, died. His surname, Sheens, was derived from the area of Edinburgh where the orphanage was located, Sciennes (pronounced Sheens by the locals).

It was common knowledge in the orphanage how Chris got his Christian name. It led to much ridicule, but the young boy was not one to rouse easily, and he took it in good humour. His calm demeanour belied the strength in the young boy. He didn't like to be pushed around and was quick to turn on his tormentors when it got physical.

The young man, who was taller and stockier than the others his age when he reached his teens, was certainly the best fighter in the orphanage. He only took a beating when the eldest boys came at him in a pack. The attacks increased, as the orphanage had three gangs and all wanted the best fighter among their number.

The new Superintendent, Mr Grimms, demanded to see the boy. 'Why have you been involved in a fight every day this week?'

Without any sense of bravado, the young Chris replied, 'I have to stand up for myself, as I don't expect anyone else to do it.'

Mr Grimms never said it, but he admired the strength, courage and honesty in one so young. He still had to punish him, but he did so in a most productive way by charging the young man with the task of organising the library in alphabetical order. The boy couldn't have been happier as old books were his great love. It was not so much the stories inside but the smell of their battered leather covers that brought with them a sense of history.

The girls in the orphanage flirted with the good-looking young man with his mop of black-hair, but he was painfully shy. This only added to his appeal, as he already had an enigmatic presence for standing alone against the gangs. He did have a long-term girlfriend of six months, but she confessed to the other girls that sometimes it was like kissing a panda as he always had a black eye.

Chris was about to turn fifteen, so it was time for him to

leave the orphanage. The day before he was to leave a young woman came to see him. It was the talk of the institute as no one had ever come to see the boy before.

'I have come to see Chris Sheens,' said the well-dressed young woman who presented herself at the front door. 'I did call to say I was coming.'

'Yes, we were expecting you,' said Mary, who did not return the young woman's smile. 'Would you like some tea?' asked the chief Matron.

'Can you make it for two please?'

'A cup for Christopher, but of course. He's a good boy, but he gets into too many scrapes.' The comment made the young woman a little uneasy.

The young woman was led into the Superintendent's office.

Chris entered moments later. 'Hello, can I help you ma'am?' he said, as he kept one hand in his hair to cover a nasty graze on his left temple.

She offered her hand, and he shook it very gently.

'My name is Katherine Kildare.'

'It is nice to meet you. I'm Chris Sheens.'

'No, you're not. Shall I pour?'

'What?' Then he saw her reach towards the teapot. 'No, please let me do it,' replied the now confused young man. Immediately, he regretted offering to do so, as it meant presenting both hands.

'The cuts and bruises on your knuckles look very painful,' said the young lady.

'I'm sorry.' This was the response that the Superintendent had asked from him after hospitalising the other boy, who had attacked him with a stick the day before. The Superintendent didn't expect the boy to apologise and, as he confessed to Mary later, he would have been disappointed if he had.

'I'm training to be a nurse, so I'm not squeamish.'

'I'm looking for work, is that why you're here? Good people sometimes come here to give us a decent start out there.' He paused. 'Forgive me ma'am. But what did you mean when you said I was not Chris Sheens?'

'I came to see you because,' she paused to compose herself, sitting upright with her hands clasped together in her lap. She drew a deep breath and swallowed hard, then said, 'You are my brother.'

The young man did not say a word as this was the most incredible thing that had ever happened to him. In a matter of seconds, the beautiful, kind and obviously wealthy young lady had presented him with the two things he had craved all his life: family and the chance to finally discover who he really was. He experienced so many sensations: happiness, shock, all resulting in such an insurmountable number of questions racing through the young man's mind that he said nothing.

'I only found out myself yesterday, so I'm as shocked as you.' She smiled and so did Chris as they looked at each other like children about to open a large, beautifully wrapped present. She burst into laughter and Chris did too, and the expression of each was so similar that neither had any doubt they were indeed siblings. Nevertheless, she asked, 'You do believe me, don't you?'

'Why would you lie?' replied the young man.

The woman got up and walked over to Chris, hugged him and began to cry.

'It's okay Sis: all will be fine now,' he said as if he had been saying those words all his life.

After a few minutes she finally pulled away and began to laugh once more, as she wiped away the tears streaming unreservedly down her face. 'It's all too much. Tomorrow I will pick you up and take you to my house . . . sorry, I mean our house,' she added joyously.

'Are my parents there?'

Katherine stopped laughing. She took his hands again in hers. 'No, but I will explain. Now, I must go and prepare for tomorrow. The Matron said they need another day to have the paperwork in order for you to leave. Then I will tell you everything . . . at least everything I know.' She hugged him once more and almost skipped as she left the room. Chris was still standing in the centre of the Superintendent's office when Mary returned ten minutes later.

'Is this a dream, Matron? Did that stick across me bonnet yesterday dislodge something?'

Mary looked at him and then the surprises continued. She lifted her hand up to his neatly combed black hair, ruffled it and smiled. He slumped back in the chair and said in a quiet voice, 'I knew it was a dream.'

For the rest of the day, none of the gangs bothered him. No doubt fearing that if one of them even brushed against him in his over-excited state, he would batter them all to a pulp – laughing maniacally as he did so. In the dining room, Suzy appeared by his side and tugged at his arm. 'Are you going off with the beautiful lady tomorrow?'

'God, yes!'

One of her beautiful green eyes released a tear. Chris put his hand under her chin, which made her embarrassed as there were others in the dining hall and most were now sniggering.

'Will you still be my girlfriend?'

'What, two girlfriends! I'm not English, yer know!' she shouted back and went to slap him across the face.

He blocked her hand. 'The lady who came today is my sister.'

Suzy's face was a combination of surprise and relief.

The following morning the young man, who had not slept, made his way to the front door of the orphanage with his packed knapsack on his back. Mr Grimms shook his hand warmly and Mary gave him a curt nod of her head before lifting her hand up to straighten his collar – he didn't mind. An hour later, having run after leaping from the bus as it turned into the Golden Mile, he stood outside the grand Edwardian house. He checked the address in his hand again and took a deep breath. Chris lifted the cast-iron knocker and dropped it down. But, he caught it before it clattered down on the wood. The young man swallowed, straightened up and adjusted his school tie. This time the clatter of the knocker loudly announced his arrival.

Katherine raced ahead of the servant to open the door. All night, she had lain awake in her huge double bed and promised herself that she would retain her composure when her brother came to call in the morning. Now, that he was standing on the doorstep, she was laughing as she leapt up into his arms. With her legs suspended in the air and her face pressed into his shoulder, she knew that she wouldn't be alone after all.

'We have the same father, but not the same mother, but this afternoon we will go and see your mother.' Katherine and Chris were now seated in the grand drawing room. They were surrounded by portraits of their family, strangers to the young man.

The maid entered. Although nineteen, she had the demeanour of a middle-aged housekeeper. She was carrying a silver tray on which sat a bone china tea-set and a plate of scones with an abundance of butter and raspberry jam. Chris stood up as she approached the table. The maid placed the tray down on the walnut table with the authority of a mother serving breakfast to her children. Having done so, she raised herself up and made no attempt to disguise the sarcasm in her voice.

'Sir, there is no need to stand up, I'm just one of the servants.'

Chris did not move. 'You're foremost a woman. Therefore, you will be treated with due respect.'

Katherine smiled as she glanced at Kirsten. The maid, who was her friend and confidant, appeared to blush as she reversed out of the room.

This time Katherine poured the tea. She took a deep breath. 'It will be painful, but we will go and see your mother together. But now, I will tell you all I know of your history.'

Chris had even more questions as he had been awake all night too, but he promised he would not interrupt her as she related their story.

'Our father was Terrance Kildare, a wealthy Edinburgh

businessman. He made his money firstly through importing cotton and later when he opened a number of millinery workshops in Edinburgh and Aberdeen. He married my mother, Mary Wilson, when she was sixteen and he was in his fifties. An unusually late age for a man to marry. But, he was known for his regular dalliances. He approached the parents of at least four women, that we know of, for their daughter's hand in marriage but they refused to give their permission. Later, he approached my mother's guardian, a Mr Alan McBride. My grandparents on my mother's side died of typhoid, and Mr McBride was a distant cousin. Apparently, he had been keen to look after her as the monthly income from her trust was useful, with him being a professional gambler and all. But, having cleared out all the money in her trust fund, he was also happened to be in severe debt to her suitor. The marriage was sealed.'

The next part of the story was clearly painful for Katherine to tell, but she felt she owed it to her brother to do so.

'While my mother was carrying me, our father took advantage—' She stopped and lifted her eyes to look directly at her brother. 'No that is not true – he forced himself on the new kitchen maid. The maid was your mother Angela; she was only fifteen. She became pregnant with you and as was the case then and sadly still is now, young women bearing children out of wedlock were put into an asylum. It was there you were born. My father wanted nothing to do with you or your mother, and he arranged for you to be raised in the orphanage and all records that may connect you with him to be destroyed.' She took her brother's hands in hers. 'Chris, I'm so sorry.'

Chris' elation of the day before was but a memory.

'It's not your fault Sis,' he said quietly.

'I feel terrible; you were born only a few months after me, yet I was raised here, in these surroundings and you . . .' she began to cry once more.

He got up and pulled her towards him. She buried her head into his chest and hugged him. He tipped his head down and rested his chin on his sister's hair. 'Your mother told you all this?'

'My father died last year and my mother passed away two days ago. The night before my mother died she told me everything. She did so because she said because she didn't want me to be left alone.'

'You won't be.'

'My mother was a good woman and wanted you to know she was sorry she never came for you once my father had died. But she confessed that she didn't have the strength to face the shame of what had happened.'

'But, you did. You could have carried on as things were. But you came for me.' He lifted her head from his chest, looked her in the face and smiled. 'Thank you, Sis.'

That afternoon they took a taxi across town to the Royal Edinburgh Asylum. They sat waiting outside the Supervisor's office while Chris' mother was being prepared to meet them.

Katherine was holding Chris' hand as a woman who was supposedly only thirty-one but who looked nearer sixty with long, grey hair was led by the hand into the room. She was painfully frail and covered in bruises.

Chris walked slowly over to the woman. He bent his

45

knees and folded his arms delicately around her, but she didn't seem to notice. He turned to the Supervisor. 'The bruises! What have you done to her?'

The Supervisor walked over to the distraught young man. 'I can assure you, we have not hurt her. I am sorry to say that the poor woman has cancer, an inoperable tumour in her brain but fortunately benign. A side-effect is that she is easily susceptible to bruising. May I suggest you remove your hand from her arm.'

Chris did so, and he saw that already a large black handprint had begun to appear.

The young man lifted his mother up in his arms and turned to Katherine. 'We're taking her home.' Carrying the woman as if she were a light bundle of clothing, he walked towards the door.

The Supervisor leapt up. 'You can't simply come in here and walk out with one of our patients, even if you say she is your mother.'

Katherine stood up and wrote some details down on the note paper that lay on the Supervisor's desk. 'These are my details and those of our lawyers, Sinclair & Sons. I have instructed them to complete the paperwork for Miss Connelly's release.'

The Supervisor continued to protest. 'I can't—'

'You can. Please, understand that her son simply wants to take care of his mother in the time she has left.'

The Supervisor was surprised by the young woman's determination, as she stood between him and the door. 'Of course I understand, but you have no authority, this is illegal, it's . . . kidnapping . . . I repeat, no one can just walk into this institution and—'

'Chris can; you just don't know my brother,' as if she had known him all her life.

Katherine turned around and followed her brother. Two orderlies were waiting for them at the main door. Chris kept walking while fixing his eyes on both of them. The Supervisor appeared behind them and waved the orderlies to stand aside. Katherine ran ahead and stepped out onto the pavement to hail a taxi to take the three of them home.

July 1936, Edinburgh

Ten years later Katherine walked into their garden where Chris was feeding his mother some broth he had prepared. His mother had not spoken a word since her arrival, but she had grown content over the years, even smiling at her son as she took a sip of soup from the spoon. However, she now had a malignant tumour in her brain.

'Chris, I'm leaving for Spain tomorrow,' said Katherine.

'Good, you deserve a holiday, but not there as the country has descended into civil war.'

'That's why I'm going. I have volunteered to be a nurse in the International Brigade, fighting the Fascists in Spain. Over 2,000 Scottish volunteers have already left these isles to fight for the Republic.'

'But why? I thought your cause was equality for women.'

'It is, my brother, but the causes are not mutually exclusive as both are a fight for liberty. As a Scot, our lives are always a struggle for freedom.'

'Then, I will go with you. But I can't leave my mother. Please wait a while.' He dropped his voice. 'She doesn't have long.'

'No, my passage is booked. In two days' time, I will depart on a ship from Portsmouth to Marseille. Your duty is here. Savour this precious time with your mother.'

The following month, Angela Jane Connelly died peacefully sitting in the garden in her son's arms, in the house where she had worked for a short time as a young chambermaid. After the funeral, where Chris, the Superintendent from his orphanage, the Supervisor from the asylum and Mary were the only mourners, he returned home to pack his knapsack for Spain. Suzy was to marry a policeman though Chris had had an engagement ring in his pocket when she told him. Good for you, he thought. He had wanted to marry her so that she would have some money from his inheritance if he died in Spain. There was nothing to keep him in Edinburgh now.

Chapter 5: Darker Realms

May 1939, Berlin

'The *Abwehr* (German military intelligence) are complaining. They say that espionage, counterintelligence and sabotage are under their jurisdiction.' Obergrüppenführer Reinhard Heydrich addressed the major, but it was not an admonishment. 'But, I do not trust Admiral Canaris and his army officers.'

The major was pleased, but it was impossible for either Heydrich or Reichsführer Heinrich Himmler to tell. Seven months earlier, Sean Ryan had blown away most of the left side of Cerberus' face and jaw. His bodyguard, Rerck, was the only person close enough to notice the facial tic that indicated his pleasure. His commander's right eye would open wider as what remained of his jaw muscle on that side of his face would contract, pulling on the nerves above.

'However, we are displeased about the London incident,' added Himmler. 'I empowered you, so that you have the freedom to activate the Alpha Wolves whenever you please. Your mission in England was a failure. I trust that no evidence implicates us in what the international press is calling the Battle of London?'

'We left no tracks. Nothing implicates us in the affair,' replied the major. Applying a white linen handkerchief, he wiped the saliva that regularly built up in the corners of his crooked mouth.

'You were also unfortunate that the accidental explosion has disfigured you so.'

'An unstable gas cylinder exploded as it was being loaded onto the train, Reichsführer.'

Heydrich glanced at Himmler before continuing. 'You have the Rogues in your sights?' asked Heydrich.

'All of them will be eradicated in days.'

'Ensure they are,' said Heydrich, as he walked away from the window leaving behind the view of the bland grey buildings that stood along Prinz-Albrecht-Straße. He took a seat in front of Himmler's desk. Neither of Major Krak's superiors bade him sit down.

The major continued his report. 'The Alpha Wolves who survived the London operation will pay for their failure along with their leader Colonel Pen–'

'We have no need of details; just have them dealt with immediately. Failure is a virus that breeds lethargy, and it must not infect the Alpha Wolves,' interjected Heydrich.

Once again, Cerberus' eyes did not betray his delight as he was convinced that neither of his superiors knew that Lenka had escaped while he was personally interrogating her. If they had, he would now be facing a firing squad in the courtyard outside.

'Once the Rogues are eliminated you will return to your objective; to undermine all opposition to the Reich before the invasion,' continued Heydrich.

'Of course, Obergrüppenführer.'

'And what of your plans to expand operations at the Fortress?' asked Himmler.

'They are ahead of schedule. I have also initiated an

additional project.'

Himmler and Heydrich both smiled, in expectation of hearing the major's latest initiative, for Cerberus had a mind as sadistic as their own.

'Along with retrofitting furnaces to existing prisons and other buildings, I have ordered new rolling-stock. These will be prototypes to test the development of mobile incineration units.'

Himmler reclined in his chair as he brought his small hands together as if in prayer.

'I have designed sealed wagons that are at this moment being constructed in our armaments factories in Dusseldorf.'

'The purpose?' asked Heydrich.

'To be used as mobile abattoirs.'

'How?' asked Himmler.

'Firstly, oxygen will be sucked out of the wagons. This alone will nullify most of those inside. Poison gas will then be pumped into the wagons to deal with any survivors. Minutes later, the gas will be extracted, and the containers will then be filled with flames.' Himmler's eyes narrowed behind his orbicular lenses, as he pressed his fingertips tighter together.

'How will you control the operation?' asked Heydrich.

'A control panel is being installed in my personal carriage. From there operatives will administer the gas, the extractor fans and fire. Throughout the train there will be a system of pipes secured to the steel plated walls of each wagon.'

'How long will it take to cleanse each wagon?' asked Heydrich, who also drew his hands together as if to join his master in worship.

'We will not know for sure until we carry out the first test in the field. However, laboratory tests indicate 15 minutes to extract the oxygen, 30 to 60 minutes' exposure of the gas and ten minutes to incinerate the bodies.'

'How will you dispose of the remains?' asked Heydrich.

'The ash will drop through the floor.'

'How?' asked Heydrich.

Cerberus dabbed the saliva building up more than usual on his uneven lips with the handkerchief. 'My design for the floors in each wagon is based on that of the release mechanism for the undercarriage of a bomber. The plates in the floor will open, but there will remain a grate that will run along the length of the floor, through which the ashes of the occupants will be sieved, assisted by the motion of the train. Of course there will be skulls and the largest of bones will remain, but these will be crushed under foot by the next cargo.'

'I have a concern. How will you neutralise the threat of combustion?' asked Heydrich. 'The Hindenburg disaster ended our entire airship manufacturing programme. We can ill afford a repeat of such an event.'

'Obergrüppenführer, the various gasses are inert and our technicians will be monitoring the entire blending process to ensure they remain so. The oxygen in the wagons will also be extracted before the gasses are pumped in, hence even if a volatile element enters the process it will be impossible for the gases to ignite.'

'Why not produce the gas beforehand?' asked Heydrich.

'Our experiments in our facility in Lake Como have produced impressive results, but it is only with a "live" experiment that we can truly be satisfied that we have identified the most effective compounds. It will be a delicate operation. But as I have said, Obergrüppenführer, once all the occupants are dead, the suction pumps will be activated for a second time to remove any gas from the wagons. Only then will propane gas be released through the pipes, ignited remotely and flames introduced to the wagons.'

Himmler and Heydrich remained silent, but their smiles indicated their sanction of the major's plan.

Cerberus wiped away the dribbles that he realised were drooling from his chin. 'If the experiment is a success, we will be able to build a number of such death wagons.'

'Do not be so explicit about their purpose in any correspondence or use that expression outside this room,' said Himmler.

'Of course Reichsführer,' replied the major.

'Is that everything?' continued Himmler.

'What I have described is merely an addition to the core mission.'

His superiors silence, again, indicated he should continue.

'Our rail engineers in Düsseldorf are manufacturing a specially reinforced frieght chassis.'

'For what purpose?' asked Himmler.

'To carry Panzers.'

Himmler and Heydrich's smiles broadened.

'It will give us the ability to mobilise our heavy artillery, in support of our troops when we advance across

Europe,' continued the major. 'It will secure the territory taken as a result of Blitzkrieg, by rapidly deploying heavy artillery to support our forces on the ground.'

'Continue, major,' said the Reichsführer, as he unconsciously began to drum his fingertips together.

'A fleet of *Eisenbahnpanzerzuge* (armoured trains), each loaded with 38-tonne Panzer tanks, can be off-loaded and ready to advance within minutes. They will be accompanied by a squadron of Alpha Wolves.'

'With the addition of your, shall we say, containment and cleansing facilities.' Himmler smiled in response to Heydrich's comment. 'We will be able to *treat* prisoners as we advance,' said Heydrich.

'When will the first tests take place?' asked Himmler.

'Three trains, including my own, will be ready to conduct the first trial next month. We are only waiting for the specially designed pumps for the main section to arrive from Amsterdam later today. We have a number of families in readiness for the test.'

'Where will the test take place?'

'My train will deliver our cargo to the Fortress and we will carry out the first trial *en route*.'

'Why the Fortress?' asked Heydrich.

'If the pilot fails, we can erase the evidence in its furnace.'

'Excellent, major,' said Himmler. 'I usually view the need for a contingency as a lack of faith in the primary plan. However, such is the sensitivity in this case that we cannot risk discovery.'

Heydrich began to drum his fingers together. 'The Fortress is becoming increasingly important to our plans. I have just received news that the laying of the additional reinforced rail tracks has been completed.'

'Now the transportation of the heavy water can begin,' noted Himmler.

'The first delivery takes place tonight, with further consignments to follow every four hours. With three tracks to negotiate the mountain, we will have over 30,000 gallons secured within the Fortress by the end of the week. Then our tests can begin.'

'Do not fail us, major, as the Fortress is essential to our plans. Remember our facility in the Norwegian Fjords? We centred a number of our operations there: the storage of the first extraction of heavy water from the town of Rjukan, while we were also conducting our experiments on poison gas,' said Heydrich. 'We were fortunate that when the aerial photos taken during the RAF aerial reconnaissance fell on the desk at the Admiralty the request to send part of its fleet to investigate was rejected' (the desk was that of a junior minister). 'However, our 'guinea-pigs' drew the attention of–'

'Ah yes, the Englander,' interjected the Reichsführer. 'When he razed the facility to the ground, the Führer made his displeasure clear.'

'A rare mistake that we learnt from with your creation of the Alpha Wolves Reichsführer,' said Cerberus, who felt no need to mention that he now knew the man was an Irishman.

'Quite so,' smiled Himmler.

Cerberus involuntarily wiped the saliva trickling from the sides of his disjointed mouth with his long, anaemic fingers – forgetting his handkerchief, such was his excitement. Knowing his plan was approved – though as always nothing was signed – he saluted both men. 'Heil Hitler!'

Himmler and Heydrich raised themselves to return the salute but quickly resumed their previous discussion – the arrangements for the Führer's first anniversary celebration of the Munich Agreement and the fall of Czechoslovakia.

When Cerberus had closed the door behind him, Himmler spoke. 'We must inform the Führer of this. It will be the greatest commemoration gift we could give him.'

'What of Cerberus?' asked Heydrich.

'You are his mentor: what do you suggest?' replied Himmler.

'He thinks we are fools if he believes we do not know that he allowed two of the Rogues to escape in Paris and leave him as the grotesque animal that we have had to endure. But, I recommend, Reichsführer, that we continue to let him think we are ignorant of the facts. Later, we will use this knowledge as a leash to restrain him.'

'A leash?'

'His mythological namesake was untethered when it guarded the entrance to Hades. We cannot afford to take that risk with *our* creature. We should wait until his prototype trains have proven their effectiveness. Then we will order Cerberus to hand over all the files he has amassed on our enemies. This must be done before his train is part of any invasion force. We cannot afford to lose such a valuable archive if the ledgers fall into the hands of our enemies. Even the *Abwehr* does not possess such an invaluable record of those who would oppose us.'

'Records that could lead to the collapse of every

European government in the weeks before invasion'
Himmler's eyes were now slits.

'The major is a master of strategy, and he may wish to use the archive as insurance if he learns that we know of the events that took place in Paris. However, if he believes we are ignorant of the facts, he will not feel threatened and will obey my orders and deliver the files. Then we can apply the leash by informing him that we know of his failure. Now, with the leash secured tightly around his neck we can use him any way we wish.'

'Do we not already have that power?'

'Total control will be required, if one day we need to root out our opponents within the German High Command.'

'You distrust him?'

'I distrust his ambition, Reichsführer; but for now let us continue to direct it towards far darker realms.'

Chapter 6: The Black Pearl

March 1939, Paris

Vodanski and Jake entered a café by the Seine, opposite Notre-Dame. Neither man had spoken to each other since leaving the Catacombs.

Chris was walking behind with Sean and spoke quietly.

'It looks like everything has returned to normal between those two. That's if normal means refusing to acknowledge the man fighting beside you. Is it just culture that divides them?'

'I thought so once. Later, I thought it was a clash of personalities, but now I think it is something that happened before we knew them when they fought together in Spain.'

'When they are with Lenka they often make a toast to a woman called Dominique.'

'I asked Lenka about her, but she said that it was for them to tell me. I have the sense that neither will.'

Samuel poked his head forward from behind one of the grand Belle Époque columns at the far end of the restaurant. Sean was the first to see him and strode over in his direction.

'If they put you behind this column because of your colour, I will raze this place to the ground.'

With the aid of his cane, the one legged American army veteran was now on his feet and grasping Sean's hand in his.

'No, I have received nothing but kindness since I arrived here, Sean. Back home I would have been tossed out with the garbage by now, but here the waiter asked if I preferred *blanc* or *rouge* with my meal. It's just that I'm not used to places like this. I am far happier away from crowds. So I asked if I could sit here, at the back.' He laughed and bent his head forward as he whispered. 'So please don't raze this lovely café to the ground, and forgive me if I sound ungrateful, but I fight my own battles.'

'I am suitably chastened, but what the hell are you doing here?'

'I'm Chris, pleased to meet you,' said the Scotsman, extending his hand. 'Please sit Samuel; the Rogues are not ones for standing on ceremony.'

But, before he could sit down Jake and Vodanski walked over from the bar. More hand shaking followed, but Samuel was glad when they finished so the blood could flow back to his fingers. He was pleased to see the men again, and their similarly tall Scottish friend, but he was surprised to receive such a warm welcome.

Samuel addressed Sean. 'I will let Jake explain why I'm I here, as I'm just an interloper.'

'You were more than that in New York. You saved our lives.'

Jake poured red wine into the glasses in front of them and placed the now empty-bottle in front of the one remaining empty glass in front of Vodanski.

Samuel pushed his glass of wine towards the Russian.

'Please, take mine, my friend. I'm not much of a drinker,' he added. Vodanski nodded to the man, as he picked up the other bottle of red. Then he hit the base of the bottle so hard with his hand that the cork popped up from the neck so the Russian could pull it out with his teeth.

Jake muttered, 'Neanderthal' glancing at the Russian.

'Once you have wiped that look of disgust from your face Yank,' said Sean, 'can we return to the hospital?' Jake took a gulp from his glass but still shook his head at the Russian. Sean continued, 'On our way here you outlined how we will reach the hospital, but not what we will do with the patients we find?'

'I have prepared paperwork to transport those we liberate from the hospital to America. Once we know who we are dealing with, I will telephone the British Embassy here, with the names, if we discover them, their ages, sex, hair and eye colour. We have up to twenty foster homes ready to take them in, but we'll organise more if we need them. Roosevelt is in on this, but I guess that is down to your friend Winston.'

'The Englishman is a mystery, inside an enigma holding a brandy glass,' replied Sean.

'The president is on board?' enquired Chris.

'He has a great respect for Britain.' Jake leant forward on his chair in the direction of Sean and Chris. 'Look, I had one short meeting with FDR. He was candid. He respects Churchill for his stand against the Nazis, but believes he's an imperialist and mistrusts his motives.'

'Well, it sounds like at least you have his confidence. But are you sure that those we rescue from the hospital will be allowed into the States?' asked Sean. 'Not only do we not know how many we will have, but we have no idea what their mental and physical state will be.'

'We can try, Sean. But you're right, many oppose letting more émigrés in, let alone those who are not judged to be fresh-faced, able-bodied children. But that's why I have been trying to open the door a little wider on our side of the Atlantic, now the door on Europe's side is closing.'

'Even American isolationists must realise that the Nazis won't stop now that Czechoslovakia has fallen,' asked Chris.

'It's not just isolationists. There are those who hate the British and would love to see Germany defeat them. You've heard of Joe Kennedy, the US Ambassador to London.'

Sean nodded. 'Irish descent, so no love for the Brits.'

Samuel interjected. 'What about the persecution of the Jews? They have a voice in America.'

'It's not the loudest.'

'But surely the American people can see the danger the Nazis pose?' asked Chris.

'Roosevelt has an uphill struggle. Even national heroes like Charles Lindbergh has gone on the radio and told the nation that it is the Jews who are the real threat.'

Samuel shook his head. 'I read it in the columns of discarded newspapers and hear it on the radio. Antisemitism, as someone said, "is a light sleeper".'

Sean topped up Jake's glass then the others. 'You have a big desk in the State Department, Jake. Are you sure you want to join us?'

'What do you think?'

'If you're captured, the Nazis will make the most of you being a *bona fide* American government official. Even if they don't, your bosses won't be happy.'

'Bollocks to Washington!'

'Good, plus you're even learning how to speak the Queen's English,' commented Sean. 'One thing, if America refuses to take those freed, I have an alternative. I have a sister in Cork who has set up a children's home since her husband died. Without giving her the details, she said she can take four, five at a push.'

'Funny, I never thought of you having a family,' said Chris. 'Does the Government cover the costs of the home?'

'No, it's all donations.'

A young, black woman, about five foot seven wearing a silver sequined dress approached the table. The four Rogues stood up when they saw her, with Chris gently lifting Samuel up by his arm.

'Sam!' she cried.

After hugging the war veteran, she acknowledged the others. 'I'm Josephine Baker. Perhaps you have heard of me.'

'Who hasn't?' replied Jake, though by the bewildered looks of Vodanski and Chris they obviously had not.

Sean turned to them. 'This lady is a star of stage and screen and is renowned across the world as The Black Pearl.'

'I have many other names, but as I'm black and an exotic dancer not all of them are nice,' replied the artist. 'Gentlemen, please be seated.'

Sean slapped Samuel on the shoulder. 'Forgive me my friend, but how did a hobo from New York become friends with a star of the music hall?'

'I used to beg outside the Plantation Club in Harlem and every night she would put a few dollars in my hat.

When I told her that I was one of the Harlem Hellfighters, she kind of made sure I never went without food when she left to live in France. We still write.'

'I'm used to powerful men wanting to wine and dine me in the hope of sleeping with me. Sometimes a lady tires of the dance. Sam, will you come and watch me perform tonight? Then I will find you a job at my club.'

'Me? But I'm a bum with one leg.'

'Now there's an image,' said Sean.

'Believe me, Sam, you are more of a man than most I have met.' She lowered her voice. 'Sam has written to me and while he has not gone into the details, he says you are helping families flee the Nazis.' She looked at the faces of the five men, and only Chris and Samuel acknowledged her words. 'I have influence. It extends into the darkest corners, but I will call on it if ever you need help.'

Jake slipped a note across the table. 'We need transport. Can your contacts help?'

The woman opened the paper and examined it carefully. 'I have a few contacts in the military that will help.' Sean then added a few items to the note.

The artist read it and looked at the Irishman. 'What are these?'

'Welcoming gifts.'

She turned to her old friend. 'Stay close to me, Sam, and be my liaison.'

Samuel smiled, tipping his head as he did so.

'I'm on stage at the Moulin Rouge in an hour so I will take my leave of you despicable Rogues. And the tension between you two,' she said, looking at Jake and Vodanski, 'is a war in itself.'

Jake laughed. 'Really, I thought we were actually getting on like a house on fire.'

'One with gas canisters in the basement,' added the Russian.

She smiled at the four men, as she helped up the war veteran. 'Look me up when you get back.' For the first time, her smile left her. 'The Nazis will throw everything at you. Take care.'

All the men now stood up. The singer and dancer shook her head. 'My, I feel like a little girl lost in a forest of huge tree trunks.'

Jake took her hand and kissed it. 'Come back to America and help change it.'

'One day, but I'm not playing to any fucking segregated audiences.'

'Quite right, and I'll be in the audience when that day comes,' said Jake.

Sean then kissed her hand, followed by Vodanski and finally Chris.

'An artist learns to read her audience. There is so much pain in all your faces, but you Scotsman you seem to want to be somewhere else?'

'It's nothing personal, I can assure you, Ma'am.'

Josephine stepped up on a chair and placed a kiss on Chris' cheek. 'Don't be in too much of a rush to leave. Life is precious; respect it.'

Chris gave her a warm smile.

Jake turned to Sean, as Josephine helped Samuel cross the floor of the café.

'The Brits are convinced Lenka betrayed you and the lieutenant. But I take it you don't, or one of you would be dead by now?

Sean said nothing.

'Christ, I've had more open conversations with the Russian Bear,' said the American throwing his arms up in the air.

Vodanski had taken another swig from the wine bottle before Sean took it to top the others' glasses up.

Josephine and her old friend exited the cafe, where her chauffeur was waiting as he held open the car door. At the same time, a party was taking a table next to the Rogues. The man who directed where the others in his party should sit, bellowed, 'Negro whore.'

Jake and Sean did not exchange looks as they placed their glasses down on the table, while Chris turned towards the man. But before any of them could act, Vodanski clamped his hand on the man's collar, wrenched him backwards from his chair and slammed the back of his head down on the Rogues' table.

The Russian bent his face down, so it was just above the man's bulbous nose. 'I do hope you have a fucking problem with me.'

Chapter 7: Jake's Story

July 1907, New York

Jake was born in Breezy Point, Queens, New York. His parents, the Frankenbergs, were German émigrés who came to New York at the turn of the century. During The Great War, such was anti-German sentiment in the country that for the sake of their children they changed their name to Flynn. Malfreda and Anton Flynn had eight sons and two daughters – they were devout Catholics – and though poor, it was a happy family. Jake was the youngest and the wildest. He got himself expelled from various schools. His misdemeanours ranged from fighting to being caught in a compromising position with a female in the school – his physics teacher, Miss Chesterfield. Eventually, he had to go as far south as Brooklyn to continue his education.

His father had secured a job in the city's Fire Brigade. This was unusual, for enrolment in the police and fire brigade was the "privilege" of the Irish, many of whom had come to New York and either joined the gangs in Hell's Kitchen or law enforcement – though the lines between the two were often a little blurred. His father was a big man, as were all his sons. With his physique and the fact that he scored top marks in the written entrance examination, he would be expected to be top of the list of new recruits. However, at the time, he was still far from certain that a

German émigré would be accepted into their ranks. Fortunately, he had many neighbours who vouched for him.

Jake excelled in all sports, though one coach noted "he had an issue with authority". He would often go hunting with his father, an excellent shot, and brothers and would fell more targets than the others put together. After a short stint as an amateur boxer, he joined the police (his father was now in a position to secure the support of even more Irish colleagues in the Brigade). However, it was not long before he was kicked out for breaking sergeant's nose for beating up a young boy he had caught stealing.

He then got a job as a stevedore on the docks of the Hudson River. He got into even more scrapes there; this time not with the authorities but with union officials from the Teamsters. It was common practice that a portion of all cargo unloaded would be 'lost', yet would be listed on the dispatch log. Jack did not view this as any of his business, but he refused to be 'part of the muscle' when a union official tried to recruit him. When the same man attempted to strong-arm him into doing so, he and two colleagues lost a number of teeth.

Jake knew the mob-controlled union would try to force him out, but he enjoyed the physical demands of his job and the camaraderie that came with such a mixture of nationalities. The docks, though heavily unionised, relied on a constant influx of new immigrants who would pay a percentage of their wage to the bosses, including a cut for the union. During meal breaks, Jake would listen to the stories of their homeland. Though he had a passion for learning more of the world, he no longer bought a newspaper. He confided in a girlfriend, 'I have correspondents providing me with daily news of international events.' The woman missed the irony and informed her friends proudly that 'she held the arm of a well-connected gentleman'.

The latest wave of immigrants were fleeing the outbreak of civil war in Spain. Franco's Nationalists had overthrown the democratically elected Republican Government, while the Communists, Anarchists and Socialists were attacking the church and committing terrible atrocities on the clergy. It was a valuable lesson for the tall blond American (who his colleagues thought to be a German immigrant until they heard his drawl). Jake learnt that in war that the enemy did not always represent all you despised. His Spanish friends were torn as they were on the whole Republicans, but many were also devout Catholics.

But, Jake's sympathies were with the Republic when he heard through his friends, as well as in reports on the radio, that German and Italian bombers were now spearheading the attacks on civilians – despite both countries signing a non-intervention agreement with Britain, France and the United States.

Jake was reluctantly dragged to Carnegie Hall by one of his girlfriends, Casey, to listen to the author Ernest Hemingway speak in support of the Spanish Republic. He only did so because that night he was more interested in the domestic affair he was having with the pneumatic redhead, who was married, than international ones. She too was enraptured by her lover, adamant that the big New Yorker came right out of one of Hemingway's books. On one occasion, when they made love, she kept shouting out

'Philip! Philip! Agghh! Philip!' the name of the lead character from his first literary success, *A Farewell to Arms.* Jake didn't care as he was thinking about her sister.

Jake had rather more in common with the novelist than the heroes of his books. He shared the author's vices of strong liquor, adventure and women and, despite being a New Yorker, hunting. Both had the physique, grit, personality and good looks to exceed in all areas. Like Hemingway and many young American men and women his age, Jake also held the belief that democracy was a natural right of any society. He also detested both Communism and Fascism, seeing both as opposing sides of a fake coin. Both publicly professed to be of the people, while their leaders sacrificed them for their personal ends. Jake would freely admit that he was no great thinker and could not abide politicians. His actions were guided only by a moral sense of right and wrong.

Despite himself, Jake was impressed by the author's passionate speech. Hemingway was also a "man of action"; wounded as a volunteer ambulance driver in WWI, he was now a correspondent for the North American Newspaper Alliance in Spain; often to be found filing reports in the midst of battle. Casey was similarly surprised that her boyfriend was perfectly willing to meet the author – a former lover. Jake was not one to be overawed by either fame or status. An hour later, amongst a throng of drinkers, the three made their way to McSorley's over in the East Village.

The author held out his large, calloused, hand to Casey's boyfriend. 'You look handy in a fight.'

'I'm a lover, not a fighter,' replied Jake.

'Both, I'd say, and nothing wrong with that,' laughed the author, as he pressed two double bourbons into the couple's hands. 'Casey says you have an interest in the Spanish Civil War?'

'It's not a Civil War anymore from what I hear, but an international one. Some of the new Spanish immigrants I work with say the Germans and Italians are waging a new form of warfare.'

'I believe it's the precursor to a new European War unless we do something. Also, there is nothing "civil" about war.'

Downing his liqueur in one mouthful, Jake ordered another round. Casey was proud that her lover was not overwhelmed by the enigmatic writer and adventurer – as her friends usually were.

'I'm keen to travel to Europe, so I may see for myself what is happening in Spain.'

'If you do, look up a good friend of mine when you get there. Her name is Lenka Haberman.'

'A nurse?'

'Far from it, she produces patients and more frequently corpses. She will take you under her wing.'

'I don't need protecting.'

'You will, more from her than the Fascists.'

A month later, Jake got a job working on a freighter about to cross the Atlantic to Europe. He arrived in Paris and stayed there for three months; it would have been longer, except having squandered the rent, he had to flee his boarding house. Those months were spent drinking in the city's liveliest bars, and, on the rare occasion when he hadn't turned a young woman's head with his good looks and charm, prostitutes. His hedonistic pleasures led to a number of fights with jealous boyfriends, overprotective brothers, cuckolded husbands and aggravated pimps who felt he was exceeding his allocated time – though the girls never complained.

He was not one of those who got caught up in the romance and adventure of the Spanish Civil War. But when he read reports in the American press confirming that the German and Italian air force were now carpet bombing Republican villages, he decided it was time to head to Madrid.

The next morning he left on the first train for the Spanish border. He threw his knapsack up onto the luggage rack and plonked himself down only to find himself facing a lieutenant and two infantrymen from Franco's nationalist army. They were returning to the front after taking leave in the French capital. Then, just as the train was leaving, Jake saw a young woman running onto the train platform with a sack over her shoulder. She threw open the door to the carriage, bundled her possessions in, and jumped in after them, landing face down on the carriage floor.

As he lifted her up by her arm, Jake found himself looking down at the most beautiful face he had ever seen. Her hair was long and straight, very unconventional, as city women in Manhattan and Paris were always doing things to their hair – bobs, curls, even crew-cuts – but the length was usually short. She wore no makeup and her skin was almost spotless. She had a few pimples on the end of her nose, as she had a habit of rubbing the back of her hand against it when she was vexed. Her wide eyes were sparkling green.

The top three buttons of her white blouse were unfastened but it was still tight around her breasts and the tail was tucked, or rather jammed, into her black skirt, in a practical but unfashionable manner. To round off her no-nonsense, country girl image, she wore a pair of climbing boots that were too big and seemed only to be held on by the overly thick mountaineering socks she was wearing.

'Want a hand, Sweet-cheeks?' said the American as he held his hand down to the woman.

'Sweet-cheeks!' snorted the unimpressed woman in English but in a very strong French accent. She rejected his hand and got back on her feet, put her sack on the luggage rack above the empty seat next to the American, turned and flopped down next to Jake.

'Oh shit!' she said when she saw the other four passengers.

The lieutenant leant forward. 'You seem ill at ease in our presence, Madam. Why is that?'

The French woman responded, while still slightly breathless, which all four men noticed as it made her chest press tighter against her linen blouse. 'I don't like to be referred to as Sweet-cheeks, nor do I like dirty bastards who keep staring at my breasts.'

'Sorry,' said Jake, as he looked at three men opposite.

They did not return his look.

The train trundled through the Parisian suburbs and within an hour it was weaving its way through the countryside. The woman fell asleep, but somehow remained upright refusing to let her head fall towards the window or towards the American's shoulder.

When the train reached the French-Spanish border, a border guard got on the carriage. Having checked that the French woman's documents were in order, he was about to return them and move on to the others when the lieutenant interrupted him. 'Give them to me.' He looked at the French woman. 'Then I will take a look in your bag,' said the officer in French.

Jake expected a feisty response, but the woman said nothing as the officer began to read the documents aloud. 'Dominique Marceau, aged 21, born Toulouse,' He then folded her identify papers and placed them inside his jacket. 'Now, your bag, Mademoiselle?' he demanded.

'You get it,' shouted the woman, as Jake realised that her way of holding her tongue was not to speak at all.

The lieutenant lifted himself up and pressed his pelvis into the woman's face as he slowly lifted her bag down from the luggage rack. The American's clenched his fists. The lieutenant tipped its contents onto the floor. A number of glass jars smashed as their contents, an assortment of jams and pickled meats, splattered her clothes.

Jake moved forward to pick up her belongings. 'Not your concern, American,' said the officer. Jake ignored him and picked up the garments that were not yet spoilt and handed them to the woman and said, 'I'm sorry.'

Dominique said nothing but stared angrily at the lieutenant.

He looked at a piece of paper and smiled as he addressed the woman, 'A Madrid address, a city occupied by our enemies.' The officer smiled as he slipped the note into his jacket. 'We need to strip search and then interrogate the Republican bitch.' The train began to move forward, but the border guard seemed eager to stay. The officer ordered him to get out. The border guard immediately jumped down onto the platform as the train began to pull away from the station.

The lieutenant turned to Jake. 'You too, Yank, get out and make your way to another carriage.'

Jake took a packet of cigarettes from his top pocket.

'I'll get off at the next station, as I'd like to join you in a little fun with her. Happy to go last if that is OK with you guys.'

The lieutenant was furious. 'We are not stripping this bitch for your amusement.'

'Fucking pigs all of you,' yelled the French woman, as one of the soldiers grabbed her by the throat.

Jake smiled at the lieutenant. 'OK, calm down. It's too late to jump off now, but I'll get out when we pull into the next station and leave you guys to have your fun.'

Dominique was struggling, but when she did manage to speak her abuse was aimed at the American.

As the train raced across the Spanish landscape, Jake leant forward. 'Sorry guys, for spoiling your fun,' but only the officer understood English. The American lifted a pack of Lucky Sevens from his top pocket and banged the base of the packet on his knee. Five cigarettes popped up, and he offered them to the men. The two soldiers, including the lieutenant, did not hesitate as American cigarettes offered a taste of glamour they had only seen in Hollywood productions. The American flicked his cigarette up to his lips and lit it in one smooth motion. The three soldiers tried the same, but only one of the infantrymen succeeded while the other two had to retrieve theirs from the floor after they had bounced off their faces. The American held out a light from his gun-metal Ronson cigarette lighter given to him by his father before he left New York. As the successful catcher leant forward, Jake connected with his jaw with an upward swing of his clenched fist. The man's jaw broke instantly. Jake had learnt the street brawler's move on the streets of Brooklyn. You would offer an opponent a light, and when he moved forward with his mouth open you delivered an uppercut. A punch to a dangling jaw would usually break it. In rapid succession the other two soldiers suffered a similar fate.

Dominique just looked at the three unconscious bodies on the carriage floor and turned to the American.

'Fuck me now!'

'But, they may wake up?' said a surprised but delighted Jake.

'Well, as long as you concentrate on what you are doing, you can knock them out again.'

Having retrieved the papers from the unconscious officer's coat Jake rolled the three soldiers out of the carriage as the train entered a tunnel. After that, Dominique and Jake made love four times. Jake had never met anyone so wild and free. Dominique made love with an abandoned passion he had never encountered before. Just as they were about to make love for a fifth time, they were interrupted by two old women who boarded the carriage at San Sebastian. Dominique didn't seem to mind, but the cold stare of the two women made Jake ill at ease for the rest of the journey to Madrid.

As the train pulled into Madrid Dominique grabbed his

hand. 'Are you coming with me?'

'No, but I will find you!'

Jake headed off to find an American volunteer unit, The Abraham Lincoln Brigade, which had African-Americans and even a contingent of British in its number. He felt obliged to join it not just because he was American, but because he couldn't speak Spanish. Dominique joined her friends in Major Talbotá's unit though it was common knowledge that the real leader was a Polish woman: Lenka. Both groups fought closely together during the coming months in what was to become known as the Battle of Madrid. Jake soon became disillusioned after witnessing the ineptitude of the Brigade's Spanish commanders. This, along with his unrelenting distrust of authority, led the American to join the more anarchic, though in battle by far the more professional, 'Lenka's Rogues'.

'This is Lenka', Dominique had said as she seized her friend in her arms when she first introduced Jake to the leader of the group. The two women had shared many adventures since first meeting three months earlier when the International Brigades first marched together into Madrid.

Everyone who fought in Madrid had heard of Lenka, including Jake. He had heard that the Polish woman was not just a great fighter, but, like him, she didn't care for the Communists or the Anarchists; she just wanted to stop the Fascists.

'I'm Jake. Mr Hemingway sends his regards.'

The tough, long-haired and wiry brunette turned and shouted to the big man cleaning his dismantled rifle in the corner, 'Just what this war needs. Another Yank coming to find himself while trying to fuck as many women as he can in the process.'

The Russian held the barrel of his gun up to the sulphur-stained sky to check the barrel was now clean. 'Let's hope this one can wipe his arse and makes it to the end of the day, unlike the others.'

'Hard cases eh? Well, we'll soon see if it's all wind and piss or you're as tough as you think you are,' said Jake.

Dominique laughed even louder. 'Lenka, Jake's a bit uptight and insecure about us, but he's my man.'

Lenka looked unimpressed. 'Take care of her, or the Russian and I will cut your head off and shit down your neck.'

'Is that the Bear in the corner?'

The Russian lifted himself up and walked over to Dominque, who jumped up into his arms. After kissing him on the cheek she released him, took his hand and led him over to Jake.

'I'm Vodanski.' The Russian was an inch taller than the American and had a bigger build that stretched the seams on the largest jacket that the Red Army suppliers could find him.

'A red!' Jake replied with blatant distain.

'A cowboy!' Vodanski retorted with unbridled contempt.

The two women looked at each other, ignoring the tension between the two huge men and embraced each other. Each man placed his weight on his front foot, adopting a solid stance to get in the first strike.

Dominique jumped in front of Jake. 'Vodanski has taken on the role of my guardian. I don't need protecting, but it's nice that someone cares.'

'I take it he wants to fuck you,' spat Jake.

'Idiot, it's not like that at all, he's more like a father, even better as mine fucked off with a sailor.'

'A sailor!'

'Don't you dare laugh; my mother drank herself to death with the shame of it.'

Vodanski walked back over to the American; his fists now clenched so tight that his knuckles were bleached white. 'Treat her badly once, Cowboy, and you will never do so again.'

'I don't need to be taught manners by a commie, and when I'm by her side she will be safe.'

Dominique sprayed her arms out like a bridge between the two men. 'Enough! I make my own decisions. And as long as I'm alive you two must never fight each other. Promise me!'

The men said nothing but continued to stare at each other.

Another woman entered, dark-haired as the others, but taller and curvier and ran towards Dominique and lifted her into the air as she hugged and kissed her.

'She made a lot of friends in the few months she was here,' said Jake but not looking directly at the Russian.

'She was her lover before you,' said the Russian.

Jake looked at him not knowing whether to believe him or not and then he looked back to Dominique.

From that moment forth wherever Dominique went Jake was by her side, even when to his fury she would run off without notice in the direction of enemy fire. Jake was in love with her, and she felt the same about him. Whenever she met any of her old friends, she made a point of dragging Jake forward. She did not pretend to be cool and aloof when he was beside her; in fact, she rejoiced in her feelings for the big American. Jake was more reserved, particularly in front of Lenka and Vodanski, each of the view that Dominique would be safer with them.

One evening, they were together up in the derelict houses guarding one of the side roads that meandered its way into the backstreets of the city when she looked up at him. 'I love you, Jake.' The American had heard the words many times before. In Chevrolets parked in front of drive-in movies and even in the last few weeks in a seedy room above a funeral parlour in the red-light district of the Rue Saint-Denis. But this was the first time he had wanted anyone to say it.

'Do you love me?' Jake fumbled for an answer. But she answered her question for him. 'Of course you do, unless you are completely dumb. You men, your emotions are just wrapped up in a ball, terrified to express how you feel. So funny,' then she climbed on top of Jake once more.

That summer, Jake along with Vodanski taught all the new volunteers how to be better shots. But, more importantly, how to maintain their weapons especially as the ones they had were inferior compared to those supplied to the Nationalists.

Most of their weapons came with the wrong calibre of bullet, hardly any of the mechanisms were greased and some were already seized up and rusty. Jake was frustrated and refused to use the Canadian Ross rifle he had been issued as it repeatedly jammed, irrespective of how well he maintained it. He also refused the German *Infanteriegewehr* 98 Mauser supplied, although it was good for its time – the end of the last century. Instead, he selected the Astra M901. It was a self-loading pistol, with an attachable butt extension and held a 20-round fixed magazine. He had prised it from the rigid fingers of a Nationalist guard's torso, to add to his two M1902 Colts with eight-round removable magazines.

Despite their inferior weaponry, they were the best unit the Republic had and were a match even for the crack units of Moorish mercenaries that Franco had brought with him from North Africa. The unit, like the others, suffered a shortage of food and clothing, but their bravery in battle was renowned. Lenka was fearless as indeed was Dominique, but the Pole, like Jake and Vodanski, always weighed up the risks. Only having done so and judging the risk was acceptable, would she advance on the enemy. Dominique didn't, she just charged at the enemy while shooting her rifle whenever the opportunity presented itself.

After each engagement, Lenka, Vodanski or Jake would admonish her for her latest foolhardy action. But she would laugh and just say, 'If the good die young, then we will all live forever.'

As far as the other Rogues knew, Jewel, the Australian nurse, had never scolded anyone. However, one day during an attack by the Nationalists she came under fire in the middle of the street. Dominique ran out and jumped into the water-drenched crater with her to return fire with the enthusiasm of a child entering a play pit. 'What you did was incredibly brave, but don't ever do that again please!'

pleaded the Australian nurse.

The following day, Dominique ran to pick up a hand-grenade that had landed in the middle of Jewel's make-shift hospital and threw it back out of the window at the enemy. This time Lenka tried to talk to her.

'You saved us all, but please stop throwing yourself at danger. You are young and believe you are indestructible but trust me, so far you have been lucky. Jake is in a terrible state worrying about you, and he's not the only one. Do you know what it will do to us if anything happens to you?'

'Nothing will, I promise,' she said and grabbed Lenka and dragged her around the room in an enforced tango. Though Jake loved to see Dominique dance, and even more so the look of horror on Lenka's face, it did nothing to lighten his mood.

'Lenka, she is driving me crazy,' confessed Jake later to the leader of the Rogues.

'That's Dominique. Naïve and headstrong, she brings life and uncertainty with her wherever she goes. It's why we all love her, for she is the child amongst the Rogues.'

'Vodanski wants to do more than love her.'

'No, he has a daughter he has never seen, and I believe she brings out some paternal instinct in that fortress of fury. But, if anything ever happens to Dominique, he will not rest until you are dead.'

'Fuck him. She is a woman, and as she says, she makes her own choices. He has no right to have any say over her life and certainly not mine.'

'Boys will be boys, I guess.'

'It's all crap anyway; nothing will happen to

Dominique as long as she wants to be in my arms.'

Jake tried to teach her how to use any available cover. 'My father taught me that in a fight, you need to think like a soldier, not a gangster.' He noticed that whenever firing broke out, Dominique never dropped to the ground. Jake continued to castigate her for being so reckless, but she retorted that it wasted too much time as sooner or later you had to lift yourself back up. He refused to give up and instead tried to teach her how to use the cover all around her, the walls, columns, lamp posts and telephone poles around them. With their next encounter with the Nationalists, she stood right out in the open street firing at an armoured car heading towards her so that she could take a clear shot. Jake managed to take out the driver and the vehicle then careered into the telephone pole, which fell on top of the car killing all its occupants. Jake was furious and when the skirmish was over he stormed over to scold Dominique, but she spoke first.

'Lucky I wasn't standing behind the telephone pole; I'd be dead by now,' retorted Dominique.

If she refused to protect herself, Jake decided he had better teach her how to be a better shot for as he once told her, she couldn't hit a buffalo's arse with a banjo.

He added, 'You watch too many Errol Flynn movies.'

'We should make a pornographic film together. We would be millionaires.'

'I don't think my mother would approve.'

She made the common mistake of firing directly at a running target, rather than ahead of it. Soon she learnt to do so, firing one metre ahead of the target for every hundred metres away they were. He told her to release the first round off as quickly as possible when she saw her target. 'Even if you miss, it will startle your opponent into moving so when they return fire there is less chance of them hitting you.' He also imparted his police training, teaching her how to manoeuvre through a building holding her revolver in both hands to steady her aim.

He tried to alter her shooting posture of pointing her pistol with a straight arm, to a more natural crouched three-quarter hip position, which she liked. To the American's relief, she listened for once. It also meant she would be in a better firing position when they fought at close quarters, which, as the enemy was taking more ground, was more frequent.

'I know you are trying to protect me, and I will listen because I want us to raise our children together.' She lifted herself up on tiptoe as Jake smiled and bent down to receive the most gentle of kisses.

'Children?'

'Of course. We will have a life after the war. That is why I'm knitting this.'

'Knitting?'

'Yes, my Grandmother taught us all how to make clothes.' She lifted up the little white hat. 'This will be for our first. I hope it will be a girl, as I will need her help to look after the rest.'

Jake appeared dazed and kept repeating the same word 'Children!' But to Dominique's delight he did so wearing a big stupid smile.

'Yes, that is why we had better enjoy ourselves and do

plenty of fucking and drinking because once we start to have children we will need to grow up.'

Jake amazed himself with how readily he took to the idea that he had never even contemplated before. 'Don't we need to get married or something?'

Dominique put her hand inside the front of her canvas trousers and then stroked her finger across the American's lips.

'You have my juice on you, so we are as good as married.'

Jake did not close his mouth as Dominique picked up the little white hat, her knitting needles and her temperamental 57mm Mauser rifle and went to take her turn at guarding the main door.

It was November, 1936 and the Luftwaffe's Condor Legion and the *Corpo Truppe Volontarie* were launching a heavy bombardment of Republican-held cities and towns, especially the capital. Much to Lenka's disapproval, Jake had packed the windows of their headquarters with books from the city's Public Library opposite. In the limited circumstances, he judged it the best option for stopping sniper fire. They could also be easily pushed aside to pinpoint and then take out a target. This became a source of mockery from the Russian. 'And they say that Americans have no use for literature.'

The night before, a mortar explosion had covered everyone with books and fragments of shelving. Vodanski held up the thick bindings of a leather-bound book with a bullet wedged in it but no longer containing any pages.

'Ah, *The Thoughts of Stalin* was of some use after all,'

noted the American wryly.

Now that the fighting was so close, Lenka decided they would all sleep in the basement. One night during an intensive aerial bombing raid on the building, Lenka was naked, wrapped in Vodanski's arms. On the other side of the room lay Jewel, who, as always slept uneasily under a blanket such was the extent of the burns inflicted on her as a child. Another six or seven volunteers were lying in various positions in the cellar; only Jake and Dominique were obviously awake and it wasn't due to the bombing overhead. They were all used to that.

'What's wrong? I can hear you thinking,' asked the French woman of her man.

'Nothing,' said Jake. Dominique knew that a man's 'nothing' was 'always a something.' She just waited, and then it came: 'That Russian lump tried to wind me up when we first met.'

'What did he say?'

'Oh, just something about that tall, statuesque beauty Martina, being your girlfriend.'

'She was,' said Dominique, who cuddled up closer to her man.

Jake had a thousand thoughts going through his mind. He was jealous, surprised, even confused, but one thought overrode all the others.

'Err, if you like we can ask her to join us . . . that's if you still want her to.'

Dominique roared out laughing, so much so that she woke the others. As Lenka and the others looked up, they saw Dominique on top of Jake, naked, but even more surprisingly considering that they could hear explosions nearby, laughing loudly. 'Men's brains are always in their pants. He wants a threesome with Martina', shouted Dominique, over to Lenka.

'Decadent Capitalist,' shouted Vodanski.

Lenka was half awake and said, 'You wanted me to have a threesome last week with a prostitute from the International Hotel, so best you shut up, hypocrite.'

She lifted her head and shouted over to Dominique. 'God has cursed us both with the affliction that we are attracted to idiots,' and went back to sleep.

Jake was not easily embarrassed, but he was then, though everyone ignored them and went back to sleep.

'Am I not enough woman for you?'

Jake smiled. 'More than enough, but talking of sex, do you always have to be on top?'

'I come that way,' she said, with a grin.

The American preferred it too, as he could look at the woman that he was in love with, but as yet hadn't found the opportunity, or perhaps the courage, to tell her.

Then he heard a whistle, followed by an enormous explosion, and everything in the room disappeared within a cloud of powdered brick dust.

The room was thick with powder and smoke, and Jake could see nothing. Thankfully, he could still feel Dominique's naked body pressing down on him. Waving his arm wildly, he saw that it was badly charred, but he ignored the pain. As Dominique's face came into view, she seemed strangely vacant; her features frozen. A warm sensation travelled down the lower half of his body. Jake lifted his head and saw blood flowing down his hips. He moved his limbs, and the pain in his legs told him that he had received multiple burns. Jake looked down, now that the brick dust was settling, but he was finding it hard to focus. He thought a sheep or some other animal must have been caught in the blast, as guts and entrails were lying around him on the floor. It must have been caught in the blast. He could see the heat rising from its innards.

He froze and looked up. 'Dominique, say something.' But her face fell on his. He moved his hands up from her hips and then his hands entered her body. He rolled her over onto what was left of her back and then her brain slipped slowly down to the floor. The back of her head and the top of her back were completely ripped off, and then he realised that the fingers of his right hand was still inside her wrapped around an organ. Days later, he realised that he had probably been holding her heart.

Katherine Kildare arrived the next day at the Rogues headquarters, the Banco de España on the Calle de Alcala near the junction with Gran Via. She found much activity as men and woman were clearing rubble and repairing the building in the aftermath of the attack. Some shook her hand, others nodded while forcing a smile. An Australian nurse, whose face was terribly scarred, limped towards her. Jewel introduced herself and offered her some tea. While the water boiled in a pan in the corner away from the others, the Australian woman told her of the young woman's death.

Katherine's first task was to treat and bandage burns to the tall, blond-haired American's arms and legs. She knew that the bandages wrapped tightly around his wounds must have caused him terrible pain, but he did not complain. He only said one thing when she finally tied the last knot, 'Thanks, Sweet-cheeks.' However, she was struck by how disengaged the handsome blond man was from his cheeky remark.

Dominique's funeral the next day was a simple affair. A hole dug solely by the American, who refused the Russian's offer of help. He then lowered her into it with his bare hands. One other, a young man by the name of Leonardo, had also died, but they were all lucky to be alive, as a large part of the floor above them was now rubble. Lenka said a few words but nothing that Jake heard. The American never talked about the French woman that he and the other Rogues had loved. Not even months later, when he was with Lenka and they became lovers for a short time. But, whenever they made a toast it was always to Dominique. It was the only time following her death that the American and the Russian put aside their hatred for each other.

Chapter 8: The Hospital

April 1939, Lake Como

Bellagio lies at the tip of the peninsula formed by the Y-shape of Lake Como. It can be reached by road, but it was already treacherous before Captain Tak (the new head of the European division of the Alpha Wolves) posted machine-gunners in the hills above. Oberleutnant Von Grese was the Senior SS nurse in charge of security of the new facility at the edge of the lake. A powerfully built woman, nearly six foot in height, whose hair was tied either side in the usual pretzel shape adopted by women of senior rank in the National Socialist Party. She specialised in keeping alive those undergoing 'processing' for as long as Cerberus required. The nurse was very proud to have been personally selected by Major Klaus Krak for this assignment.

However, there had been an abundance of guinea pigs upstairs so her specialist medical abilities had not been required. But her thoughts were also on the call from Cerberus that morning ordering her to make arrangements to relocate the operation by the end of the week, 'as it had served its purpose'.

Since the renovation of the building, her core task was to ensure that no uninvited visitors got past the newly erected steel doors to the Institute – a task she had carried out with the utmost diligence until that evening.

Oberleutnant Von Grese marched across the hall to admonish whoever was hammering on the door. When she threw the door open, she found four men, all over six foot tall, dressed in German uniforms – splashed with blood – standing in the porch. She did not flinch, until she saw that the tallest of the men had been using the face of one of the sentries posted at the main door as a knocker. The man let the dead guard slip from his hand as he bent down towards the SS officer's upturned face. In a broad, unfettered Russian accent, he addressed the granite-faced woman.

'You in charge?' he demanded, in the little German he knew

'Yes,' she said as she went for her Walter P38, while about to cry out to alert the guards. Vodanski grabbed her by the throat and with one abrupt wrench of his wrist, snapped her neck. He lifted her up to his full height and propelled the dead woman through the glass window of the staff office to his left. Such was the power of the man that her momentum carried her straight on through the office until her head crashed through the exterior window of the building. She came to a stop with her head and left thigh impaled on two large fragments of broken glass wedged in the base of the now windowless frame.

'The Neanderthal has the subtlety of a brick,' said Jake, without looking at Sean or Chris as they followed Vodanski into the main hall.

The Russian had calculated that a loud noise would bring the guards into the hallway and away from the patients. However, as there was not a scream or a gunshot they would in all probability arrive without their weapons cocked. He was right.

In the space of two minutes, the four heavily armed but ill-prepared Stormtroopers that appeared on the landing at the top of the main staircase lay piled up below it in the hallway. Next to them were the eight bullet-riddled guards that emerged from the doors on either side of the corridor. Jake, the best shot, had killed half of them. He did so expelling an even distribution from both Astra M901 'rapid-fire' automatic pistols, managing to leave two bullets in the magazine and one in the chamber of each.

Without a word, the four Rogues took different routes to check the house in accordance with Jake's plan.

Vodanski made his way towards the back of the building, and there he found a number of local staff hiding in the kitchen. He shouted 'Avanti!', but the kitchen staff were already falling over each other trying to get through the back door before he reached the second syllable.

Jake reloaded his weapons from two of the eight magazines secured to the back of his black leather belt and, his back to the wall, edged his way up the staircase.

With his Webley in his hand and his Enfield No. 1 Mk VI slung over his shoulder, Sean went to secure the left wing of the house. It was empty apart from a number of sealed canisters that were labelled *Gift* (poison) and *Entflammbar* (inflammable) all marked with the universal logo of a black skull and crossed bones below.

Chris made his way down the stairs into the basement. After checking a number of rooms, in the farthest room at the end of the corridor he discovered a middle-aged, thin, bespectacled man cowering under a table. His doctor's coat was covered with various coloured dry stains and in the top left-hand pocket were a plethora of pencils. Chris quickly assessed the man. He was badly organized, so therefore had to be in charge to be allowed to get away with his dishevelled appearance (the Scotsman had learnt much from Sean on how to read people). The abundance of nasal and ear hair and the morsels of breakfast caught between his yellow teeth indicated that the man was not concerned with matters beyond work.

'You are the head of this institute?' asked the Scotsman, in hope that the doctor would understand.

The doctor replied in excellent English. 'Yes, but please do not kill me for I am doing good work here.'

'Good work? Well, then you are very fortunate that it's me that found you. If any of my friends upstairs had got to you first, your brains would be all over the ceiling already.'

The doctor could barely control his shaking hands, as he pressed them against the table top to raise himself up.

'You have to protect me. If I am killed all my work here will be lost,' he spluttered.

The Scotsman pressed on. 'If I'm to save you, I will need to understand why your "good work" is so important. But be quick about it, as my friends could arrive at any minute.' A rattle of gunfire erupted from the floors above the two men. It was followed by screams and then an equally terrifying silence.

The doctor required no further prompting. 'Yes, anything. What do you want to know?'

'Why set up your operation here?'

'This is one of the most beautiful locations in the world; who would look for such a facility here?' He lifted himself onto the dining room chair. 'A few years ago we established a similar facility in Norway. As with our Italian neighbours here, the Norwegian Government had no idea what we were doing.' He clasped his hands together to steady them. 'But, it was razed to the ground by a man who Major Krak calls The Englander. The major is obsessed by the man.'

Chris thought of the Irishman upstairs and wondered if he knew that the Nazis had had him in their sights for some time.

'That barbarian put our research back over a year.' He shook his head. 'I just cannot understand this primeval reaction by some people to deny the progress of science.'

'Why not build this in your homeland? Surely, you would be safer from attack there?'

'Of course, but the British have a network of spies and even informers,' he replied, shaking his head. 'Here, you could say we are hiding in plain sight. We also have good information that British intelligence in Italy is non-existent.'

'Tell me more about this "good work" you are carrying out here.'

'My work and that of my colleagues is to free the world of the burden of those who have, how shall I term it . . . genetic defects. Yes, that would be the correct phrase in English. Yes?'

'You mean find a cure?'

The doctor laughed. 'Why waste resources on a cure? No our aim is to expedite their termination, but on a grand scale.'

Chris shuddered as if a cold wind had swept across his body.

'Our experiments are in their early days. Firstly, we are

sterilising those with defects, including medically castrating the male patients.' He pressed his hands down on his knees. 'Though I must say, the results have been most encouraging, yes, very encouraging indeed. We monitor their deaths.' The doctor's excitement continued to build. 'Take one example: death through malnutrition.'

Chris swallowed hard as he looked at the tied-up carcass of a hog and a heap of plucked chickens piled up on a table next to the sink in the corner of the room.

'The staff record the age, sex and general health of each patient on an hourly basis right up to their last gasp,' the doctor continued, as if he were presenting his findings in a lecture to fellow academics. 'Our experiments are not solely based on the denial of food and water; we are also developing drugs. These are administered through various channels: in their food, airborne through vents in some of the rooms here and even through a separate water filtration system built solely for our patients.' He started to rock backwards and forwards a little in his chair. 'Once again, our experiments have yielded some exciting results.'

'Your experiments are carried out . . . on–'

'Yes, the sub-humans upstairs. They all have some mental or physical defect, which means they serve no purpose to society, until now. They are all twins; well, until we began our experiments.' He chuckled. 'With twins you can carry out a live comparative when introducing drugs to one. So you see that through our work these mutations are making a valuable contribution to mankind.' He smiled.

The doctor stretched his hands out wide, as he leant forward. 'Just imagine it. One day we will be able to eradicate not just the Jews, but all sub-humans. Perhaps even one day, when we have no further need for their labour, the Slavs. Just imagine it. An Aryan society, a *Volk* populated only by strong, able-bodied men, women and children. Here, we are stretching the very boundaries of intellect and technology and combining them as no advanced society has ever done before. We are not confined by borders as our aim is to mould mankind into our image, promoting only the healthy elements, united by traditional values of work, family, service and order. So now you understand why you must protect me so my work can continue, and I can report my findings to my masters in Berlin.'

Chris managed to swallow. 'You carry out . . . these experiments . . . upstairs?'

The doctor's voice trembled with excitement. 'No, we sometimes inject our patients upstairs on the ward, but that is only to subdue them. It will only agitate them if they see what we do to the others, and there is no point making further work for ourselves. No, we carry out our experiments away from the other patients.' He grinned. 'Behind me,' and he swung around as if he were a ringmaster in a circus unveiling a prop for a new act and pointed at the huge door of an industrial fridge. 'This is the most exciting aspect of our research. In there we inject adults, children, even foetuses in the womb, with strains of leprosy, typhus and other viruses. We have also pumped various gases into this specially converted room and again recorded how long it takes our guinea-pigs to expire.'

Chris held back the vomit that shot up into his throat.

The doctor was positively gleeful as turned back to address Chris 'Until we adapted this place, our tests on those with mental and physical disabilities were, I am ashamed to say, embarrassingly primitive. In Norway, we attached a rubber pipe to a truck's exhaust and pumped the carbon dioxide in to the occupants sealed inside, but now . . .' He spun around to look admiringly again at the steel door. 'On the other side of this we are also experimenting with new, more efficient poisons. We have developed a new strain of hydrogen cyanide; Zyklon B, we call it.'

The doctor rubbed his hands and released them to give a little clap. 'The Americans created it as a pesticide, but we have enhanced its potential.' Chris tried to talk, but his mouth was too dry. 'I have no doubt that our scientists in Berlin will discover it one day. However, once I inform them of our findings it could bring our cleansing programme forward by years.'

Finally, Chris managed to swallow. 'Wh–'

'I understand your astonishment. It works like dry ice. You place it on the ground and as it dissolves the poisonous gas rises. It is fascinating to monitor the survival instincts even amongst sub-humans. Many times after completing our experiments with the gas, I have opened the door behind me to find our guinea pigs piled up in a heap. They climb up on the dead bodies desperately trying to escape the gas.'

Chris wanted to scream but was able to control his rage and though his mouth was dryer than he had ever known, he spoke. 'Yes, I understand now.'

'Good! Good! Not since my meeting with Major Krak some three years ago, have I had the opportunity to discuss my work with anyone.' The doctor reclined into the wooden kitchen chair and grinned until another burst of gunfire erupted above.

Chris' mouth began to moisten now he knew what he had to. He stared directly at the startled doctor. 'Did you actually believe I would understand the butchery you are carrying out here?'

The doctor woke up to the danger. For the six months he had been in charge of the facility, he had issued instructions to those upstairs, and no one had once objected; in fact all of them seemed genuinely impressed.

'Please, do not fear for your life. You seem to be an intelligent man and physically you are a prime example of the Aryan model. We recognise those who possess Aryan traits of physical perfection and intellect and we will enlist them in–'

'It's not my life I fear for, but my sanity,' Chris said as he lifted his revolver.

'I thought you would understand, as you appear to be a reasonable–'

'My friends above us have spent their lives fighting people like you. I'm an innocent compared to what they have witnessed. But I doubt they have ever encountered anything like this.'

'But, you misunderstand me. We are civilised people who are mastering the latest advancements in science to–'

'You are abusing science. The fact that you attempt to rationalise your barbarity only shows the insanity of it all.'

'But you said you were different to your friends upstairs who . . .' The doctor was jolted by more screams from above.

'I am different to my friends. I am not as sharp or as astute as them. They can size up a situation and take the appropriate course of action almost immediately. Whereas I need to understand everything before I act, so that's why I listened to you.'

'That is a laudable and scientific approach, so you will let me live as I–'

'Need to continue your "good works"?' Chris placed his forefinger on the trigger. 'But, once I've assessed the situation I usually reach the same conclusion as that of my friends. They would have spread your brains all over the wall behind you as soon as they walked in, but it's taken me longer to reach the same conclusion.'

The doctor raised his hands. Chris emptied the six chambers of his Enfield No 2. Mk I revolver at point-blank range into the doctor's hands as his face exploded behind it. At that moment, Sean burst through the door, Webley gripped firmly in his hand. He looked at the faceless man without hands wearing a medical coat and sitting on a chair.

'Are you okay Chris?'

'No. I think I just had our first glimpse of the gates of hell.'

Chris walked over to the metal door that reached up to the ceiling and lifted the metal locking bar. He eased the door open. It was pitch black inside, but the mephitic smell of rotting meat finally made him throw up. As he wiped his arm across his chin, he flipped the light switch on beside the door. Inside were twenty or more bodies lying motionless around the huge cell. Some of the eyes were bulging while others had burst. Their faces were fixed in horror and their bodies contorted into unnatural positions. Chris knew that in their final moments, the violence of their struggle had resulted in limbs tearing themselves from their sockets. Many had fragments of flesh in their hands as they had torn at their necks in desperation as the gas burnt into their throats.

Without turning to look at Sean, Chris said softly, 'Now, we have passed through the gates of hell.'

Jake stepped onto the landing at the top of the staircase. To his left a door flew open. A Stormtrooper appeared poised to release a stream of machine-gun fire. Jake grabbed the barrel of his gun and deflected it upwards. Chunks of plaster cascaded down on the men. The American pushed his automatic pistol into the man's mouth and uploaded one shot.

The American grabbed the hair of the Stormtrooper, now with no back to his head. With his pistol still in his mouth, Jake used the corpse as a shield as he stepped into the room. A further burst of machine-gun fire was fortunately absorbed by the dead Stormtrooper, before the American unloaded two shots into the man crouched behind a settee. The first bullet went through the middle of the sofa puncturing the man's left lung and sending his head up above his hiding place. The second bullet removed most of the second Stormtrooper's cranium.

Now that Jake was sure the room was clear, he looked around and spotted on a desk in the corner an empty grenade used as a pen holder and a radio transmitter. He checked the radio was operational and, satisfied that it was, he edged back into the corridor.

Jake could hear whimpering coming from the room at the end of the hall. When he and the others surveyed the building before entering the house minutes earlier, this was the part of the house where the lights were brightest. Jake had told the others that when they entered the building he alone would take the upstairs – for if there were hostages he did not want the others to crowd his aim.

Jake entered the starkly bleached white ward, where he was met by a nurse standing behind a boy holding a scalpel to his neck just under a metal collar. The boy was skeletal in appearance, almost lifeless making the taut chain securing him to the bed redundant. The nurse was screaming in German, but Jake wasn't listening. Having continued to walk forward he was now where he wanted to be, with his boot beside a tin chamber-pot underneath the nearest bed. Without flicking his foot back, he kicked the receptacle across the aisle of the room. It hit the metal leg of the bed to the right of the nurse. Instinctively, she turned her head towards the metallic sound. Despite the lead shot embedded in her brain, she stood upright as blood oozed from the inch-wide wound in her temple. Jake ran across to grab the boy, as the scalpel dropped from her hand, and she followed it to the floor.

Vodanski entered the room. Both men stood silently in the middle of the ward, trying to absorb the horror before them. The room held four teenage patients, three boys, two of whom appeared to be twins, a young woman and the boy in Jake's arms. All had severe curvatures of the spine: no doubt a birth defect that had led to their selection as guinea pigs by the Nazis. All were chained to their beds by a foot-long chain. They lay in clothing that was as soiled as their bed sheets. The room reeked of industrial-strength chlorine.

Jake peered down at the boy's emaciated body and vacant eyes. 'I swear if I kill a hundred Nazis before I die it will not be enough.'

Vodanski said nothing but ground his teeth as he continued to scan under the beds with his revolver.

Sean and Chris entered the ward. They too were struck by the pungent smell of heavy-duty disinfectant. When they saw the conditions of the beds, they knew that it was for the benefit of the staff rather than the patients.

Jake placed the boy back down on a clean pillow on another bed. He thought of Lenka and focused on the mission.

'There's a radio transmitter down the hall. Let's make a list of the details of these poor kids, ages, sex and descriptions so London can fill in the gaps in the travel documents.'

Vodanski heard muffled crying coming from a room at the end of the ward. He ran to the door, leapt into the air and kicked it straight off its hinges. The Russian aimed his revolver at the six nurses and three doctors standing petrified inside. On the table in front of them was the naked body of a teenage boy chained by his limbs to a table. His mouth was still clamped open, and his eyelids were pulled back and pinned to his cheeks and forehead.

'I won't shoot you, I will just tear you each apart with my hands,' said Vodanski. He meant it as he wedged his revolver into the back of his trousers.

'No,' said a voice behind him. It was Chris.

'Do we just let them go?' asked the Russian.

'Let's search them for keys to the chains. Then, we will lock them up.'

'Where?'

'There is a place downstairs,' said Chris.

'You're too soft, my friend. What then?'

'I'm throwing away the key.'

Having torn the keys from a nurse's belt, Chris had released the patients from their metal collars when the deafening sound of whirling propellers could be heard. The room became a blaze of white light, as one by one all the windows began to explode around the room.

Chapter 9: Deadlier than the Male

April 1939, Paris

Lieutenant Amelia Brett walked uneasily down the stone stairs of the Catacombs guided by the light of the torch in her hand. Her unease only increased when she reached the bottom and saw the rats semi-submerged in the pools of water that bathed the labyrinth of tunnels. The only light, apart from the beam of her torch, came from a few lit clumps of stalks smouldering in the metal cone-shaped grills hanging on the damp walls.

The British officer made her way along the tunnels, frequently flinching when a rat leapt from the air shafts and landed with a splash in the pools that circled her stilettoes. The damp odour made Amelia cover her mouth and nose with a linen handkerchief. She tried to navigate the rainwater seeping through the stone above into her hair and avoid brushing against the lime mould on the walls. As she edged her way around a flooded bend in the tunnel, she saw a dim light at the end of the passageway. The entrance to the core of the ossuary was framed by two stone pillars with diamond-shaped figures on a black-painted background. Beyond that, she could see skulls and bones piled on top of each other in the form of pyramids.

She stepped between the pillars and into the catacombs that contained the bones of six million Parisians and the woman she sought.

'I had hoped to find the rats chewing on your carcass,' said Lieutenant Brett, shining the torch directly into the woman's eyes.'

'I like the scarf,' replied Lenka, trying not to squint.

The British officer immediately lifted the cashmere wrap higher to cover the scar on her neck.

'Why here?' continued the English officer, as she directed the beam of the torch towards the skulls on the walls. She returned it to the pale, drawn face of the woman at the end of the room. It was the woman she wished she could kill with the Enfield Mark Two nuzzled in the pocket of her navy mackintosh. The lieutenant gripped the handle of the pistol even tighter before she spoke. 'This godforsaken place has been your base for over six months?'

Lenka lifted her head up but did not show surprise. 'It was the one place I could think of, where I would be surrounded by those who could keep a secret.' She was pleased to register the disgust on the officer's face. 'It was a limestone quarry, dug so that the Roman invaders could build statues to their gods. Later it became a cemetery and now, apart from me, it's abandoned. If the Nazis take Paris, they will probably turn it into an underground tavern.'

The officer lashed out with a kick as two rodents launched a pincer assault on her heel. 'Spare me the history lesson. How can you stand it here?'

'I don't have a choice; I have more to fear from the living than the dead.' Lenka tightened her finger on the butt of the Browning that lay on her bare stomach beneath the blanket. 'I take it you are here to kill me.'

The lieutenant's eyes narrowed. 'Only my duty to my

country prevents me from doing so,' she said, as she involuntarily caressed the safety catch on her pistol. 'We know Sean and the other Rogues are attempting to free some patients from a supposedly Nazi-operated facility on Lake Como-'

'We?'

'The Admiralty. But we don't know if they have succeeded and I have been sent to find out.'

'How would I know?'

'We provided you with a state-of-the-art transmitter, the Whaddon Mk V11. The receiver has two-way communication up to 800 km.'

'Useful above ground, but I'm twenty metres under it. Not exactly the best place to make radio contact.' It was a lie, as Sean had run a copper wire along the wall of the stairs up to an air duct by the main entrance. However, she had heard nothing from the Rogues since they left Paris.

'Arrête, c'est ici l'empire de la mort,' said Lenka, nodding to the black letters above the stone arch where Amelia was standing.

The lieutenant raised the torch up to the words on the plaque above the entrance and read them out loud.

'Stop! This is the empire of death.'

The lieutenant turned the light back towards the almost alabaster-coloured woman lying on the boxes at the end of the cell covered by two blankets. 'Sean must believe you are not the traitor, or he would have killed you, but I know it is you.'

Lenka looked at the officer without expression. The officer stayed by the entrance of the cell as she spoke.

'Sean may believe that Jocky was the one who told

107

them everything when he was tortured. But, I never trusted you.'

Lenka's eyes remained unhesitatingly on the officer. 'If you believe I am the reason you carry that scar, and you are here to kill me, get on with it.'

The lieutenant pulled the dark blue scarf higher over the scar on her neck. 'I am here to deliver a further message from London. The Nazis have a train loaded with men, women and children, and it is soon to leave Berlin. We believe the destination is the facility described by Sean as Himmler's Fortress.' The lieutenant pulled her wrap a little tighter around her neck. 'But as Cerberus is your master, of course, you already know that.'

'You expect me to pass this information to the Rogues so that they will walk blindly into what is clearly a trap?'

'That is all I know, and whether or not it's a trap does not make the risk to the families any less. Will you deliver a message to Sean and the others if they return?'

Lenka ignored the question. 'Why do you think they say that women are more deadly than the male?' The lieutenant said nothing. 'It's because we have to be. Males are by their nature bigger and stronger, so we use our wits to survive. Meanwhile, men's brains become dull due to lack of use.'

'I have no interest in your kitchen sink philosophy.'

'Ah, sweet virginal English rose. You play the part that butter would not melt in your mouth. It won't – it will curdle. I can tell you have your hand on a gun in your coat pocket, but you will not kill me. Instead, you will manipulate the weaker sex with your looks and guile to do your dirty work for you.'

'Believe me, I have thought of little else than killing you, but I have my orders. The mark on my neck is because of you. It is you; you, a dirty filthy whore who manipulates the men around her, not I.'

'Envy is not what I feel for you, you cold, heartless bitch. I'm glad we have nothing in common. We are of the same sex, but that is it. True, you have opportunities that I never had. I was never allowed the opportunity to be sweet or innocent. I was born in a pit. To escape, I had to climb out using anything I could.'

'It is easy to imagine how you survive. Your vices are your tools. You are no more than an animal. No morals, no dignity, as base in nature as the rats that surround you.'

'I use sex to survive. It's my defence. I have also used it to find solace in good men's arms at night just to grab a few hours' sleep in safety.'

'I am not a priest; what interest have I in your confession?'

Lenka laughed. 'A confession! To you! I'm telling you this because you, my pure little English rose, you use your sex to hurt and destroy. You have no humanity. I bet no one has ever told you what a vile fucker you are. I just wanted to be the one to do so and look at you in that shallow porcelain face of yours when I did.'

The lieutenant's hand once again involuntarily touched the increasingly damp scarf now clinging to her neck. 'Do you think that the ramblings of a whore mean anything to me? My life is one of honour, of decency and respect for traditional values; everything that you ridicule and try to tear down.'

Lenka could feel her fever draining her once again. But

her finger was now resting on the trigger of the revolver beneath the blanket 'You hide your scar behind your scarf. I once had a friend who carried far worse injuries, but nothing could hide her beauty.'

'You are a conniving bitch in the service of the Nazis. Sean, Churchill and the Admiralty will soon see I am right about you, and when they do, I will be there when you are hanged by your scrawny neck.' She tightened her hand on the handle of the revolver inside her rain coat. 'And when I pick my man, it will be for love. If I want security, I'll buy a dog. They are smarter than men.' As the lieutenant turned to make her way back up to the stairs, she looked icily at Lenka. 'They can also detect the scent of a bitch.'

Chapter 10: The Rage of Dragons

April 1939, Lake Como

'You were right, Sean: one big fucking trap,' said Jake, who was lying on his back covered with fragments of glass. Without uttering a word, the four Rogues ran to lift the children from their beds and dive to the floor, shielding them with their bodies while snake trails of bullets punched into the walls around them.

'But, I was wrong about how it would be sprung,' shouted Ryan. 'I thought they would be lying in wait for us at the dock or on the road in. I didn't count on an aerial attack.' The V1 prototype twin rotor Focke-Achgelis Fa 223 *Draches* (Dragons) continued to circle and strafe the hospital with machine-gun fire.

'The Alpha Wolves have access to the best equipment that the Nazis have to offer,' yelled Jake, lying face down but supporting his weight so as not to hurt the young woman. Around the room lay the corpses of the nurses and doctors who had frozen with the first burst of gunfire.

'I only have one plan a day. What now?' shouted Jake.

'Clip the fuckers' wings,' replied Ryan.

'I count four. Two on the attack; two circling,' shouted Vodanski, who was crouched down by one of the empty window frames, with one of the twins wrapped tightly in his arms.

'Let's lure them to the dock,' said Ryan, as he lifted

himself up, along with the other twin.

A Model 24 *Stielhandgranate* stick grenade, thrown from the open doors of one of the *Draches*, came through the empty window frame and bounced across the bare wooden floor. The explosion was followed by a blinding flash of light.

'They intend to erase all the evidence along with us,' shouted Ryan. His ears ringing, he scanned the room and was relieved to see that the children were still alive. 'We have to get the children out.'

Chris scooped up the twins, while Jake lifted up the other boy. With both hands free, Vodanski began to empty the magazine, containing 25 cartridges, of the Fedorov automatic rifle at two of the *Draches* as they swept towards the hospital.

'We are here to help you,' said Sean to the young woman. But she looked vacantly up at him. He gestured that he was about to lift her over his shoulder, and this time the girl nodded her head once. Chris scrambled over and handed his Enfield rifle to Sean, as he tightened his grip on the twins in his arms.

With a further burst of fire, Vodanski blew the windscreens out of the two approaching *Draches*. As the gyrocopters weaved uncertainly towards the hospital, the other three Rogues seized the lull in the attack and ran behind the Russian towards the staircase.

One of the Stormtroopers in the specially adapted three-seater gyrocopter lobbed another stick grenade through the shattered window. Vodanski dived towards the landing just as the floor of the room collasped behind him. Face down on the landing, he felt the heat on his back, just before a raft of plaster ceiling panels collapsed on him extinguishing the flames. He was deafened by the blast as he scanned the landing for more grenades. The exterior wall beside him collapsed, nearly taking him and the stairs with it. Then Vodanski watched as one of the *Drache*s came hurtling through the wall of ward behind him.

The pilot of the downed aircraft, now hanging out of the first floor of the hospital, frantically attempted to undo his seatbelt. The man's skin began to blacken and blister in the flames, as he desperately tried to stem the flow of blood from the bullet hole the Russian had made in his neck. The downed *Drache* exploded. Burning embers shot backwards towards another helicopter that was strafing the building once again with machine-gun fire. Fragments of metal ripped through the flimsy canvas body of the second gyrocopter, with one rupturing its fuel tank. The pilot attempted to steer the aircraft away and avoid the same fate as the other gyrocopter, but having veered away it disappeared in a yellow and red cloud that rained flaming metal.

Vodanski leapt over the burning banister into the hallway as bricks and tiling continued to bounce off him like confetti.

Outside the burning building, Ryan passed the young woman very gently to Jake, taking account of her severely curved spine, and then began to provide covering fire. Cradling the four children, Jake and Chris set off on a run towards the dock. Ryan was thankful that Chris' Enfield was one of the first with a free-floating barrel, as he was able to lodge it against his right shoulder without worrying about the pain from the recoil affecting his next shot. He cursed the metal pins in his right leg. This time they restricted him from reaching any of the outbuildings.

Ryan alternated his fire between the two remaining gyrocopters, while the American and the Scotsman zigzagged their way towards the lake. As the circling *Draches* swooped down towards them, a grenade was launched from one and a stream of machine-gun fire erupted from the other.

'Jake, the flare-gun,' shouted Ryan. Jake and Chris must have heard him above the explosives as they split in opposite directions and disappeared behind two of the six stone outbuildings.

An Alpha Wolf in full uniform and black iron face mask abseiled down the rope dangling from the helicopter towards the wooden dock. As he did so, he aimed a further stream of machine-gun fire in Jake's direction. But as he hit the wooden platform, it exploded, blowing him back up into the body of the *Drache* above. It too, was now a ball of fire spinning round with its twin, three-bladed propellers screaming in rage as the teeth of its collapsing rotor-gears attacked each other.

Jake dug up the flare gun that Sean had buried. The Irishman had also hidden Tellermine 29 anti-tank mines under the dock – having tightened the trigger mechanism to increase their sensitivity – as the first of the abseiling Alpha Wolves had just discovered. The American took advantage of the darkness and, with the young woman in his arms, crept to the end of the dock. Before he reached the quay, he placed the young woman gently down behind a wall. Jake carried on, and once at the end of the dock, he stood up and, having reloaded the flare-gun, he fired it into the air. Like a moth to a flame, he waited for the fourth *Drache* to launch an attack. Within seconds he heard its blades screeching as it swooped down and began to strafe the dock with machine-gun fire. As the quay disintegrated, two Alpha Wolves began to abseil down ropes dangling from the gyrocopter.

Jake crouched down and reloaded. He jumped to his feet and fired the flare gun once more, this time into the oil barrels on the end of the dock. Following the explosion, a wall of flame rose up into the path of the fourth *Drache*. The pilot managed to steer the gyrocopter away from the leaping fire just in time, but flames licked its dangling ropes which caught alight. One Alpha Wolf tried to climb back up. The other released the rope and landed perfectly on what remained of the dock. But as he did, he triggered another of the mines. Like a toy soldier in the hands of an angry child, his head and limbs shot off in various directions.

With his boots aflame, the Stormtrooper above continued to clamber back up towards the *Drache*. The flames caught hold of his trousers, and he screamed at the pilot who was desperately trying to cut him loose. The Stormtrooper lifted his machine-gun up and released a burst of gun-fire into the fabric and steel tubing body of the *Drache*. The pilot steered the helicopter away from the dock and within seconds it exploded, adding to the burning flotsam surrounding what was left of the quay.

'Interesting!' said Ryan, having limped across the open ground in the darkness to join Jake.

'You are the master of understatement, Irishman,' said

the American, with the young woman once again cradled in his arms, as he looked at the burning wreckage and bodies surrounding them.

Ryan turned to Jake. 'They are in full uniform.'

'Meaning?'

'Cerberus has made no contingency for failure.'

'You mean for surviors?'

'He believes that with this kind of firepower, he can't fail.' Sean turned to smile at Jake. 'He's getting reckless.'

'I don't find it reassuring that the lunatic feels he longer needs to restrain himself.'

Ryan suddenly lifted his head up to the darkness. 'Can you hear the rotors? There's another one of those bastards up there cloaked in the darkness.'

A fifth *Drache* announced itself by launching piercing beams of light in search of the Rogues.

Ryan emptied the magazine of the Enfield No. 1 Mk VI towards the *Drache*. As it swooped down, two more Alpha Wolves began their ascent down the ropes from the gyrocopter. Chris must have seen it too, as he was returning fire from his position by an outbuilding; which the Nazis had turned into a crematorium. The gyrocopter swooped down towards him, like an angry wasp turning on its attacker.

Vodanski leapt over the dry stone wall and landed in between Jake and Ryan. The American lifted the young woman over to the Russian. 'Don't drop her, dumbass.' Jake turned to Ryan. 'Give me cover.'

Chris saw the *Drache* swooping towards them as he hurried both the boys into the stairwell in front of the newly installed reinforced steel door. He reloaded the

Enfield revolver, and hoping to divert the on-coming gyrocopter away from the outbuilding, he ran out into the open.

With Jake some twenty metres away, both were now directing gunfire at the gyrocopter, with bullets shattering the cockpit windscreen, but the gyrocopter continued towards the outbuilding.

Two men hanging below the *Drache* swept just above the heads of the other three Rogues. As it shot passed, Jake threw the souvenir grenade from the radio room up through the open door of the cockpit. It clattered along the floor of the cabin.

Metres from the outhouse, the two Alpha Wolves released the ropes and landed perfectly, to roll along the ground and back up into a firing stance. Above them, the pilot panicked as he felt the grenade roll up against his foot. He dived out of the aircraft into the darkness. There was only a single scream, as he landed straddling a stone wall fracturing his pelvis, the shock killed him.

Despite the fact that the aircraft above them was without a pilot and was falling towards the outbuilding, the two Alpha Wolves aimed their machine-gun fire at the American. As Jake launched himself backwards off the wall, bullets hit in his left thigh and hip.

Ryan's crystal blue eyes scanned the terrain. He saw the last of the *Drache*s collapse onto the stone outbuilding. The aircraft landed on its side, like an injured hawk with one flapping wing as one propeller spun wildly. He heard the cries of the boys coming from under the collapsed steel door in front of the body of the *Drache* and below the rotating blade. Then he saw the silhouette of two men armed with machine-guns leap up onto the metal door and then over to the right, Chris, framed by the flames of the hospital, trying to lift himself off the ground.

'Chris!' screamed Ryan, but his friend was already on his feet and sprinting towards the men firing their machine-guns into the collapsed door and the boys below.

As the two Alpha Wolves pumped streams of lead into the collapsed outbuilding, Captain Tak turned to the corporal. 'Work your way behind the other Rogues. I'll finish those below and join you,' he yelled through the iron mask. As the corporal leapt from the sloping door into the forest, Captain Tak saw the man running towards him.

The four reptilian figures rose from the flames of the lake behind Vodanski and Ryan. The men in wetsuits crept up the beach silently in their bare feet, passing the six half-naked corpses – the guards the Rogues had surprised on the beach an hour earlier, after they moored their boat. Now close enough, the scuba-drivers launched themselves at the backs of the Russian and the Irishman. Vodanski heard the sound of wet rubber twisting and turned to meet the first of the attackers with a punch to his throat, smashing the man's trachea.

Ryan also heard the sound of something being unsheathed. He spun around in time to parry the knife before it sliced across his throat. The Irishman wrenched the weapon from the scuba diver's wet hand and drove the extended blade through the glass of the man's diving mask, into his left eye socket and down through into the cortex of his brain.

A third assailant launched himself at Vodanski. The

Russian caught him in a bear-hold, locking the man's arms. Still face-to-face, Vodanski released his hold, swung his hands up his attackers' back and up over his shoulders and clasped them together across the man's throat. Though the Alpha Wolf was the strongest of those in the European unit, he was unable to stop the Russian from repeatedly jerking his head back until his spinal cord snapped.

Ryan grabbed the fourth attacker's arm and forced the knife back in and up through his neck. The Irishman swung his other hand up smashing it into the butt of the handle. The six-inch silver blade disappeared into the scuba driver's skull and once again shattered the glass of a diving mask – this time from the inside.

Out of the darkness, the blade of an SS dagger entered Vodanski's back. Before it went more than an inch, the Russian had leapt forward, spun around and seized the corporal's wrist and pulled him towards him. As the eighteen-stone man was lifted off his feet, Vodanski smashed his forehead onto the iron mask covering the bridge of his nose. The flat metal armour plate was pushed so far back into the corporal's face that it broke his nose. It did not halt the Alpha Wolf's assault, however, and he swung his knife up towards Vodanski's throat.

Ryan seized the German's arm with his hand. In turn, the Russian brought his elbow up and smashed it down into the iron mask. This time it sent the splintered bone in his nose and the fragments of his shattered cheekbones into his brain. The two Rogues had already turned away in search of Chris, Jake and the children before the corporal's lifeless body landed on the ground.

As Chris ran towards the collapsed outbuilding above the twins he saw the head of the Alpha Wolves assault force standing astride the rubble. Despite the desperate whirling of the steel blade above he could hear the twins' screams coming from under the steel door. Then the man who was mercilessly pumping bullets into the steel door beneath his feet to quell their screams turned to look at him.

Though it was open ground between the Scotsman and the Alpha Wolf, Chris did not hesitate. He continued to run towards the Alpha Wolf as he trained his fire on him. Chris fell to his left with his front under him, as the first bullets tore into his chest and legs. He rolled over to his left in the darkness – remembering Jake's advice that if you're hit get out of the line of fire. As he lifted himself back up a second burst of fire kicked up the earth to his right. After Chris had taken only a few unsteady steps, Captain Tak released a circle of quick bursts of machine-gun fire. Chris' legs gave way under him for a second time as the power of the two bullets entering his shoulder spun him in the air. This time he rolled over twice to his left, before dragging himself back up. As he did so, he desperately tried not to cry out as a result of the pain in case it gave away his position – he had also learnt much from Vodanski

Chris was only a few metres away from the boys when three bullets hit him in quick succession. The first scraped his forehead. The second ricocheted off the socket of his left eye removing his sight on that side. The third shattered two ribs, before collapsing his right lung. Despite the pain, and being barely able to breathe, he was close enough to throw himself into the gap under the collapsed steel door and the stairwell.

He managed to roll onto his back to be met by the next barrage of machine-gun fire pounding off the metal frame above him. A cluster of bullets penetrated the half-inch-thick metal panel, tearing open his right cheek. A bullet ripped into his stomach and came out the other side, ricocheting off the iron grate and clattering down the stairwell beneath him. Chris could hear the terrified screams of the twins pinned below as a bullet ripped through his chest. The remaining wall that propped up the metal door – stopping it from completely squashing him and sealing the boys in below – was starting to crumble under the weight of the vibrating helicopter. Chris turned his head to peer through the grate and was met by the boy's terrified faces. To his relief, through his one eye he could see that despite being covered in dirt and surrounded by black smoke they were not injured.

Bullets zinged and snapped against the steel door, and though Chris could no longer move the upper half of his body, he had only received flesh wounds to his legs. He began to work his legs towards the thick cross panels of the door. With what strength he could muster he started to push the steel door upwards, as bullets tore indiscriminately through his body. Chris turned his head once more towards the frightened, blackened faces of the boys. Rivers of pale flesh appeared, etched by tears, as the boys stared up through the iron grate at the injured man trying to save them.

'When I tell you, get out!' pleaded Chris. 'Drag yourselves up . . . ,' he gasped, 'and run as fast as you can.' Whether the boys understood him or whether it was survival instinct, they both started to crawl towards the gap between the metal door and the entrance to the stairwell.

Chris was able to bend his knees, and his feet were only inches from the centre of the door. He began to press his legs against it and slowly lifted the steel door enough so that the two boys were able to crawl out. 'Don't move until I say . . . or the bastard . . . will cut you down.' He controlled the pain in his voice as two bullets burst into his chest. The blood that dripped through the grate onto the stairwell became a steady trickle.

Chris had no idea how many bullets had hit him. He could barely see out of his eye, but he knew he had made enough room to place his boots against the door. With an almighty effort, Chris very slowly straightened his legs and the top of the door began to rise.

Above him Captain Tak continued pumping bullets into the pitted and holed door below, but was oblivious to the sounds of the rotor blade flailing the air now inches from his head.

Having dispatched the four scuba divers, along with Tak's corporal, Vodanski set off at a run towards the collapsed outbuilding, as Ryan limped along behind. Neither man had a weapon, a bullet had disabled the Enfield's firing mechanism and Vodanski's revolver was empty.

When Tak saw the two Rogues running towards him, he turned his automatic weapon on them only to find it was empty. Without the noise of his machine-gun he could hear the blade whistling above him. To his horror, he realised he was being raised into the air – but it was too late.

Chris gave the steel door one last push and managed to

straighten his legs as he did so. The top third of Captain Tak's head flew into the air, quickly followed by a middle slice still with the black iron mask attached. The slice of the next blade severed the little that was left of his head at the neck, before his torso fell on its knees on top of the metal door.

'Now!' screamed Chris, as both boys scrambled out of the stairwell and ran frantically towards the two Rogues heading towards them. Vodanski and Ryan swept the boys up in their arms just as both of Chris' legs fractured and the steel door crashed down on him.

The four-metre-long steel blade fell still. All that could be heard now were the crackles of embers spat out by the fires consuming the dock and the hospital.

Sean placed the twin in his arms down beside him, as Vodanski did the other. Jake limped uneasily up to them, holding the girl and the other boy by their hands. All looked down at the bloodied face of Chris. The twins fell to their knees beside the man who had saved them and wept. Sean knelt down on one knee next to his friend.

'Is that you, Sean?' asked Chris, as he raised his hand out.

'It is,' as Sean grabbed his friend's hand.

'It's time,' whispered Chris.

Chris released his grip as he began to pull a blood soaked envelope from his jacket. He pressed it firmly into Sean's hand.

'Put this . . . to good use.' Chris then clasped Sean's hand tightly in his. A few seconds later his grip relaxed, as his eyes froze.

The three men did not move and said nothing as they looked down at the still and broken body of their friend: the most selfless of the Rogues.

Chapter 11: Death Crawls to the Surface

May 1939, Paris

Jake was making his way from the British Embassy to meet Sean and Vodanski in a café opposite the Hôtel de Ville. He was beginning to dread Paris; every time he arrived it heralded more bad news. The headlines on the newsstands screamed '*axe du mal*' (Axis of Evil). To the rest of the world's surprise, and to the horror of most, the Nazis and the Russians had signed a Non-Aggression Pact. Germany now had free rein to march into Western Europe whenever it liked.

'Fucking Cossacks! You can't trust them; they will always stab you in the back,' said Jake, when he reached the bar looking directly at Vodanski.

'Fucking cowboys!' replied the Russian. 'Still afraid to lift your heads up and look the Nazis in the face.'

'When we do look an enemy in the face, we don't turn away till they are down,' countered the American.

'Some would say that the fact that you two are speaking is progress,' noted Sean dryly.

The three watched a paperboy weave in and out of the tables, innocent of the terror his cries of the front page headline were inflicting on the diners around him. Sean turned to look at the Russian to gauge his reaction to the news. 'Still with us?'

'I'll be alone facing the Nazis when you're all dead.'

Sean was not surprised by his answer. It was the same for all of them, no matter what the rulers of their countries did – no government was the master of a Rogue.

'I have asked the Brits to arrange temporary accommodation for the children,' continued Jake.

'Change of plan,' replied Sean. 'My sister has set up an orphanage and she will take the four children if we can get them to Ireland.'

'So why have I been pissing around with the Brits all morning? I guess now I have to change the travel documents too?'

'No need, a friend has taken care of it,' said Sean, referring to Si Kaddour Benghabrit.

'Sometimes, Sean, you treat us like the enemy,' snapped Jake.

'It's more to do with a mistrust of London,' said the Irishman.

They took a table, all three sitting with their backs to the wall, as the waiter took their order. A few minutes later their breakfast was laid before them, and Sean began pouring the contents of a bottle of cognac into the three black coffees.

'Still don't trust the Brits?' said Jake, continuing the conversation.

'Just the odd one or two.'

'I never met a Brit that wasn't odd,' commented the American. 'Well, my morning at the Embassy was not a total waste. Bridgette had left a message from Lenka for us.'

Before they left Paris Lenka had instructed them that when they returned, they were not to come to the Catacombs but to go first to the British Embassy and await further messages. Having arrived in the city the night before and delivered the children to the Mosque, the three men spent the night in an underground bar in the Rue Saint-Dennis.

'Cerberus is loading his train with refugees and transporting them to a recently adapted medical facility on the outskirts of Berlin,' continued Jake.

'The Fortress?' asked Vodanski, turning to Sean.

'That would be my guess,' replied the Irishman.

The men heard the maître de loudly greeting a couple who had entered the café. Josephine was wearing an extraordinary bright scarlet-coloured fur coat. The bulging eyes of the head on the fox fur wrapped around her neck gave Sean the impression that the creature had suffered a heart attack as it tried ro escape. Holding her arm was Samuel. He wore a stylish black homburg and though he was draped in a sombre black fur overcoat, underneath it he wore a light blue pinstripe suit.

'He must have the same tailor as Winston,' commented Sean.

'Gentlemen,' said Josephine, when they reached the table where the three men were now standing. 'As I said the last time, I feel like I am entering a forest of tall trees,' she said, smiling and exposing her immaculately white teeth. Her smile disappeared as she remembered their last meeting. 'The Scotsman?'

The forlorn faces of the last three surviving male Rogues gave her the answer.

'I only met him briefly, but Chris was a kind man,' said Samuel. 'Does he have any family?' Jake shook his head

'No, but four children are here because of him,' replied

Sean. 'That is why we need your help once again.'

Vodanski pulled two chairs over to the table. The two French government officials who were about to sit on them decided to eat at the bar.

'Your injuries tear at you, my friend,' said Samuel, noticing Jake flinch as he took his seat. The two bullet holes in the American's thigh were starting to heal, causing the skin to contract and pull at his wounds when he moved. Samuel also noticed the Russian grimace when he rested his back against the back of the chair. The Irishman's right leg and shoulder also seemed to torment him even more. 'How much more can you all take?' asked the war veteran looking with concern at the three Rogues.

'If we were masochists we would be in our element, but sadly we did not go to boarding school,' smiled Sean.

'You should be on the stage with that delightful Irish wit,' laughed Josephine.

'We will be, in a cage in Berlin if the Nazis get hold us,' said Sean.

Josephine scanned the men's faces. 'I will do all I can to ensure you are not top of the bill at the *Überbrettl*,' replied the woman. Her smile disappeared. 'What do you need?'

'Transport,' said Sean as he pushed a prepared note across the table.

'For the children to reach England?'

'No, that is being arranged.'

'Then, where?'

'In the opposite direction. Berlin.'

Fifteen minutes later, having agreed what was needed, Josephine and Samuel and the three Rogues said their goodbyes.

Jake kissed the performer's hand. Then, placing his hands on Samuel's shoulders, he said, 'I have to ask, why are you dressed like you're off to court?'

'My fault,' interrupted Josephine. 'Sam is my bodyguard, but I want everyone to know that he is not just an employee but also my friend.'

Samuel smiled as he looked up at the Irishman. 'I like my garb. When you drag yourself out of the gutter you want to make sure that the world knows you have arrived.'

Sean turned to them now. 'You know that the Nazis will punish anyone who helps us, so trust no one.'

'Even you, Sean?' asked Josephine.

'Especially me,' smiled the Irishman.

Vodanski took the woman's hand and lifted it to kiss it.

Releasing her infectious smile once more, Josephine stood back. 'When we are free of the Nazi menace we must meet again. When we do, I'll show you a city that knows how to dance,' said Josephine before breaking into laughter. 'Though it had better not include a gentlemen's "excuse me", for I fear what would happen if anyone tapped any of you on the shoulder.'

The Russian shook the war veteran's hand. 'Samuel, the crazy Irishman is right for once. If Germany invades, Cerberus will seek you both. Get the first flight to that shithole you call America; hide in the hills with your countrymen and don't come down until we Russians smash the Nazis.'

'I lost a leg defending what you call "that shithole", but come and find us one day, my friend, and I will show you what a magnificent country it is.'

'Sam, you will have to go alone as France is my home now,' said Josephine. She looked at the three Rogues and wondered who, if any of them, would be alive if they ever met again.

When the taxi reached Avenue du Général Leclerc, they found the Catacombs surrounded by the Gendarmes. Sean ordered the taxi driver to keep going and park around the corner on the left. As they drove past the crypt they saw a body being stretchered out of the oak doors of the grey stone building.

As Sean lifted himself out of the taxi the metal pins holding together the bones in his right leg and shoulder tore angrily at his muscles; the pain barely registered such was Sean's anger. Jake and Vodanski placed their hands inside their coats on their weapons in readiness. The taxi driver glanced up at the deep scar on the Irishman's cheekbone as he raised himself up and then at the pain on the American's face in his rear view mirror.

He swallowed hard before speaking. 'Can you pay me now please?'

'Why?' asked Vodanski leaning over the front seat towards him.

'If you go into the ossuary, in the state you're all in . . . you may never . . . come out.'

'Good point,' said Vodanski, as he pressed some francs into the driver's hands. 'But, do not concern yourself about me. I will be fine.'

Jake turned to the Russian sitting beside him and caressed the trigger of the Browning in his jacket pocket with his thumb.

As Sean made his way across the street towards the body on the stretcher, he could tell from the curvatures of the sheet that it was a woman. Then he shouted 'Merde!', as he pretended to slip and stumble into one of the Gendarmes causing him to topple back into the lead stretcher bearer. The body fell out from under the linen sheet onto the ground. Sean looked down. The dead woman's face was wrapped in blonde hair, but not enough to hide the deep abrasions to her face and her broken neck. A number of the Gendarmes began shouting angrily as they pushed Sean away. The Irishman continued to wave his arms feigning that it was an accident. He listened intently to the report a police officer was giving to his superior. Finally, he was forced back behind the police cordon, but having learnt what he needed, he returned to the taxi.

Jake beat Vodanski to the question. 'Is it Lenka?'

'No, from the hair I believe it was Lenka's friend Bridgette. The bastards gave her a good going over before killing her. I overheard one of the Gendarmes say that a witness had seen another woman being dragged away.'

Vodanski looked over his shoulder at the three men who had just pulled up in a black Citroën Traction Avant 15CV and parked opposite the entrance on the right-hand side of the boulevard.

Sean knew what the Russian was thinking. 'They'll have seen my little performance, so no point pissing around here any longer. Let's join them.'

Vodanski got out and began to walk towards the men in the unobtrusive black vehicle, as the taxi sped away. Jake turned to Sean: 'Can you take care of the French without killing them all.' Sean nodded. 'OK, then I will go and extract information from our friends over there before the Bear kills them all by breathing on them.'

Sean made his way back across the road and jumped into the driver's seat of the ambulance, just as the driver was about to get in. 'Not one fucking word or you're in the back,' said Sean, pointing the barrel of the Webley at the man and indicating him towards the passenger seat. A few seconds later Ryan drew the vehicle alongside the black Citroën, obscuring it from the Gendarmes on the other side of the road, who were still taking statements from the crowd.

The three grey-faced men in the car had not moved as the two large figures, matching the descriptions of the American and Russian Rogues, marched towards them. However, the three Alpha Wolves inside the Citroën had their hands on their Lugers. The occupants of the vehicle remained composed, perhaps confident in their superior numbers and firepower, and that the two men approaching them would not be so stupid as to do anything with the Gendarmes so close. Their nonchalant expressions disappeared when the ambulance pulled up alongside and the siren went off just as the two Rogues reached their vehicle.

The Russian smashed his fist through the side window, landing it squarely on the driver's jaw. Hours later, the driver still held that expression while the mortician was picking glass out of his face in the morgue. The other two were luckier – at first – as Jake aimed his revolver at them, having flung open one of the back doors and squeezed in beside them. Vodanski opened the driver's door, pushed the lifeless body of the driver onto the passenger seat with his boot and jumped in. He turned the ignition key startling the engine into life. Releasing the handbrake, he took the wheel, turning the vehicle into a side street. Sean followed the black Citroën and parked the ambulance behind it. He smiled at his reluctant passenger before knocking him out cold with a left hook to the jaw and then gingerly eased his right leg out of the vehicle.

Vodanski turned his head and pointed the seven-chambered Nagant M1895 at the two Alpha Wolves behind him. 'I'll kill one of you now unless you tell me where the Polish woman is,' he said matter-of-factly, as if he were asking them the time.

'You stupid pig-fucker', replied the man sitting directly behind him.

The Russian grabbed the man by the back of the head, lifted him over the passenger seat and began smashing his head into the dashboard. Meanwhile, Jake pressed his M1911 single-action semi-automatic pistol into the eyeball of the other Nazi sitting in the backseat next to him. The American calmly addressed the man. 'I suggest you tell us where the Polish woman is, or the dumb animal in the front seat will rip the top of your skull off and eat its contents with his fingers.'

Captain Touvier, the recently appointed Head of the French section of the Alpha Wolves, was equally unfazed as he pulled the SS Eickhorn Ground Rohm SS dagger from his sleeve and swung it upwards towards the American's throat. Jake blocked it with his right arm, still holding the gun, forcing the blade up into the roof of the car. He followed up by swinging his left elbow up into the captain's cheek dislocating his jaw bone. From inside his trench coat, the Captain released a second knife from his belt with his right hand, but Vodanski locked the Nazi's hand in his, fracturing his wrist.

With the siren still wailing and Vodanski's foot still revving the engine Jake made no attempt to muffle the Nazi's distorted screams. He pressed his gun once more against Captain Touvier's eyeball.

"Tell us where Lenka is, before the bear starts eating your brain?'

'Fuck Russia! Fuck America! Fuck you all!' spat the German officer now in English, despite his broken jaw.

'Good, now we know you can speak English,' said Jake, knocking out the man's front teeth with the butt of his revolver.

Sean appeared at the window. 'Will you pair of pricks stop fucking around and find out what they have done with Lenka.'

Vodanski said something in German as he produced a knife from his leather belt. The Alpha Wolf stopped swearing and for the first time he looked terrified. The Russian seized him by his sweat-soaked hair and with the man's SS knife he began to cut off his nose.

Ten minutes later, Vodanski reversed the black Citroën and parked it by the bank of the river. Leaving the engine running, he stepped out of the driver's seat and stood beside Sean and Jake. He placed his hand through the shattered window and crashed the gear lever into reverse. The three Rogues could still hear Captain Touvier's screams coming from the locked boot of the vehicle as it shot backwards off the jetty into the water. Now that Captain

Touvier had confirmed that Lenka was on Cerberus' train bound for Himmler's Fortress, the three men set off to the Gare de L'Est. None of the Rogues looked back; their focus was on the battle to come as Vodanski flung the nose over his shoulder into the once more sleepy waters of the Seine.

Chapter 12: 'A Mayhem of Rogues'

June 1939, Strasbourg

'Now that we are on the night train to Nazi Germany, are you going to tell us how we are to cross the border and intercept a heavily guarded train set to leave Berlin in five hours?'

'There should be a helicopter waiting for us at the border.'

'The note you gave Josephine?' asked Vodanski, leaning forward clearly eager to fly again.

'She proved she has influence in high places when she secured us a boat to get across Lake Como and the papers for all of us to return to Paris.'

'Don't forget the incendiary devices you mined the dock with,' added Jake.

'If anyone knows the right people and can secure us a new fun ride for our friend,' said Sean, raising his eyebrows at Vodanski, 'it will be Josephine.'

'There's only one letter difference between friend and fiend,' responded Jake, fixing his eyes on the Russian while making no attempt to lower his voice.

'There are only four letters in the difference between hero and arsehole,' said Vodanski equally loudly, his eyes locked firmly on the American.

'There are no heroes here, just two suicidal lunatics and a rational Yank. It goes without saying that no way am I getting in one of those flying death traps again, and certainly not one flown by this dick,' said Jake, tipping his head towards the Russian.

Vodanski looked sternly at Sean. 'As with all Americans, when they say it's not worth saying, they will say it anyway. The Cowboy is running for cover again, but are you with me, Irishman?'

'No choice,' replied Sean, who continued cleaning his dismantled Webley on the unfolded napkin on his lap. He grinned at Jake. 'Rational my arse, you're far too stupid to run away. So tell me, how will you reach the train?' asked Sean.

'I'll jump on a horse, hi-jack a truck or leap up an old woman's back. However I do it, I will have more of a chance of reaching the train than you two lunatics in a metal coffin.'

Four nuns entered the carriage at Frouard. The Mother Superior relaxed and opened her Bible, while the others sat uncomfortably staring towards the windows.

It was dawn when the train pulled into Gare de Strasbourg. The Mother Superior turned to the men.

'Thank you for not swearing, as you are clearly the type that do.'

'Your kind words are quite overwhelming, Sister,' replied Sean. Jake smiled, while Vodanski continued to look impassive, as they lifted down the nuns' luggage from the rack above them.

'You are Irish?' asked the nun again. Sean nodded. 'So I take it a Catholic,' she continued.

'A terribly lapsed one, Sister.'

'Something tells me—'

'You mean the good Lord, surely,' interjected Sean.

She smiled. She was used to mischievous boys, though the novice nuns appeared shocked at the man's cheek. 'My intuition tells me that where you are going will be dangerous. May I suggest you take confession before you go?'

'I have much to confess, Sister, but it would delay us until Christmas.'

'You must seek forgiveness.'

'There are some sins that even the good Lord, if he exists, will not forgive.'

Two French military officers with flying wings on their lapels were waiting on the station platform.

'Gentlemen, here are your papers and the aerial maps as requested,' said the smaller of the two French pilots. Then, he stepped back and pointed proudly towards the fragile construction mounted on a trailer fifty metres away. 'And here is the Breguet-Dorand Gyroplane, the first of its kind in the French air force. We have installed an additional seat as instructed.' He turned to smile at his colleague, who continued the briefing.

'Can I say, gentlemen, that we are honoured that such experienced flyers as yourselves have volunteered to take the gyroplane on its first successful test flight.'

'First successful test flight?' repeated Jake, releasing an exaggerated laugh. Sean groaned, while Vodanski's eyes widened as he sprang into a trot as he headed towards the gyrocopter.

The smaller officer added, 'As instructed we have

removed any markings.' His voice remained enthused as he added, 'Though all the previous prototypes left nothing to identify what they were, let alone the country where they were manufactured.'

Sean's mood was not improved when he saw the dark green flying machine being pushed off the back of the trailer. Its rails slid down two metal ramps, guided by a number of French soldiers. Jake was almost as delighted as the Russian. 'Sean, I'll miss your ability to seize any challenge, no matter how lost the cause.' He laughed even louder. 'Anything you want me to say at your eulogy?'

Sean watched the smaller of the French officers run up to the Russian, who refused the parachute he offered to him. The Irishman looked at the one now placed in his hands by the other Frenchman. 'Ah fuck it, perhaps the penguin was right and my best bet is going to confessional,' he said as he too handed it back.

The Russian returned to the group and was as excited as either of the other two Rogues could remember. 'Are you ready to look death in the face, Irishman?'

'I'm tired of looking at the bastard,' grunted Sean.

Jake secured a map from the officers and set off in the direction of the French border post. He noticed that one customs officer was happy to assist those without the proper papers, as he was resting on a brand new battleship grey BMW R12 motorbike. Following the exchange of a large number of notes, Jake mounted the motorbike and flashed his passport at the delighted official. Jake pulled up alongside the others. He shook hands with the two officers. 'You are not going up in the machine?' asked the smaller one.

'No, if man was meant to fly in that,' he looked at the flimsy aircraft, 'God wouldn't have given us a brain.'

Then he shook Sean's hand and gave Vodanski a V-sign. 'I hear Churchill turns his hand the other way and uses it as a Victory sign. I use it in the old-fashioned sense,' said Jake, slipping on a steel helmet.

Vodanski looked at Jake's new purchase. 'German shit, built for a five-year-old. Don't start crying like a baby when it throws you, Cowboy.'

Before fixing the strap on the helmet, Jake checked the two semi-automatic Astras tucked in the holsters under his brown leather jacket. Then he extracted the extension butts of each from his backpack and threw them onto the ground. 'Well, it looks like we are approaching the end. They will be waiting for us armed to the teeth.' Neither Sean nor Vodanski spoke as they were now examining their weapons. 'We could always go back,' smiled Jake.

'And abandon Lenka and the others on the train?' replied Sean. 'Cerberus has the measure of us; he knows none of us could live with ourselves if we did.'

Jake smiled again as he buckled the straps from the backpack across his chest and tightened the leather belt containing eight pineapple grenades under his brown leather jacket. The American kicked the starter, immediately firing up the two-cylinder engine. 'Do you remember the collective term Jocky coined for us in Amsterdam?'

Sean smiled broadly at the memory, but as Jake pulled away it was Vodanski who answered. '"A Mayhem of Rogues".'

Chapter 13: Memories

June 1939, Berlin

'You must have enjoyed your brief time as my guest,' said Cerberus, as he opened a small, oblong, walnut box decorated with an open-winged eagle holding a *Hakenkreuz* in its talons. He turned its contents towards Lenka. 'Yours, I believe,' he said as he picked up some of her toe and fingernails and dropped them one by one back into the box. His right eye bulged as he picked a pair of pliers up from the table and lifted them up to her face. 'Now what can I extract from you this time?'

'You fu . . .' but before she could finish, Rerck tightened his hand which completely enveloped her throat.

'You have a foul tongue, Jewess,' said the major, as he wiped globules of saliva from his twisted lips. 'It flicks at me as one would expect from a serpent.' With one hand, his thin, elongated fingers began to untie the gold ribbon wrapped around a folded red cloth on the table. He spread the cloth out to expose an ivory-handled cut-throat razor. 'I have removed tongues before, but never a woman's.' Cerberus nodded at Rerck.

Lenka bit down hard on Rerck's fingers as he forced them into her mouth but he locked her jaw, forcing it open with his other hand. As the colossal bodyguard clamped her tongue with his thick sausage-sized fingers, she attempted to block out the pain to come.

She thought of all the laughing children she had
protected in the orphanage. Of Olen giggling, as she
flopped into the snow, flapping her arms like a child as
she created a snow angel.

The pressure of Rerck's hand and the resultant pain caused
Lenka to lose control of her thoughts, releasing more
painful memories.

Dominique's vacant stare came to the foreground as
she lay motionless on Jake's chest after the dust from
the explosion settled. Leo's serious face appeared, as
he stood in front of her on the Sleepy Armadillo and
presented her with a paper lion. The boy faded away
as Jewel's shocked expression turned to delight when
they first met and Lenka held her tightly in her arms.
Her smile became that of Ursula, as she hugged her
and kissed her on the cheek in Amsterdam for the last
time.

Peering through the windscreen of the gyrocopter Ryan
could see Cerberus' train. It now had an engine at each end,
to help it manoeuvre the four heavily laden wagons and
Cerberus' carriage through the mountains. In the middle of
the train was an open platform where two sub-machine
guns were mounted. Ryan tied the rope he had requested to
be delivered with the helicopter to the landing rail, and the
other end around his waist. He looked at the train ahead as
it slithered slowly up the steep pass, and his thoughts turned

to the faces that stared at him when he closed his eyes each night.

The horror on his mother's face as she watched helplessly as his father and brother were murdered. Her tears were replaced by Leo's unrestrained laughter as he lifted the boy into the air on The Sleepy Armadillo. Leo's giggles fell silent as he lay motionless in the snow. Then his lifeless eyes were replaced by the look of resignation on Major Booth's face as he wrote a last letter to his wife at a desk in a Dublin hotel. The major's head became Jocky's, but it was upside down as he was hanging from a hook, his body torn to shreds. Jocky's empty eye-sockets were filled by Tóth's as the boy ran back to throw his arms around Sean's waist in the Cafe Griensteidl. Magdalena's head appeared above her son's shoulder. She said softly, 'If you have to choose between us, save Tóth.'

Olen jumped up in front of them, as they faded into the background. The little woman was outside the orphanage, waving, tears flowing down her face, as he drove the motorbike out through the open gates. As her face became smaller, Jewel's face materialised looking vacantly at him before she slowly fell back onto the carpet of snow in the Berlin alleyway. Sean peered down and was met by the angelic expression of Cassandra also staring lifelessly up at him, as she lay on the stone steps of the altar of Saint-Gervais. A bowed head of brown hair came into view, and as it lifted he could see it was Ursula. Before she could speak, Paul's frightened face eclipsed hers, only for him to turn his head around and cover her, as bullets punched through their bodies. The last face was the pained one of Lenka, looking up at him in the Catacombs as he held her tightly in his arms.

From the moment the gyrocopter first lifted into the air, Vodanski's tremendous strength was all that kept it from spinning out of control as its engine was far too powerful for its flimsy frame. As he steered it downwards towards the engine at the front of the train, he thought of those he had loved, only to lose.

His wife, as she stood heavily pregnant outside their wooden shack. Hesitantly she returned his wave, as if he were a stranger that had embarrassed her into acknowledging his greeting. He thought of his daughter whom he had never seen; her face was that of Katalina as he had carried her through the snow-covered forest outside Kiev – a child who he did not realise was already dead. Vodanski smiled at the thought of Jewel's exasperated expression when he tried to lift a patient without limbs into a bed by his head. His thoughts were then of Ursula, laughing as she hugged him in Amsterdam just before she set off with Paul. His smile disappeared, when he thought of how her youth had cruelly fooled her into thinking that she and her young man had a future.

Jake saw the double engine train struggling up through the pass ahead. The American had held the throttle of the motorbike open since he first heard the gyrocopter buzzing overhead minutes earlier. He thought it surprising that the aircraft had not reached the train before him. But when he saw that it zigzagged in flight like a drunken albatross, he was amazed it was still in the air. He could see the rear engine of the train and undid the strap and flung the helmet into the dense forest. His thoughts turned to those he had lost on a journey that first started in Madrid.

He remembered Dominique's delightful laugh when she straddled him that first time on the train. Her same unrestrained laughter when a few months later she mounted him once again, this time as more than lovers – only moments later for her limp body to slip down his bloodied arms. The memory of Jewel, when she cradled his face gently in her hands as she pleaded with him not to seek vengeance following Dominique's death. He thought of Ursula when he opened the door in Amsterdam, to find her now a young woman. Finally, he thought of the look on Chris' face, a look that accepted it was time to die.

Cerberus unhurriedly sipped his Earl Grey from a china cup, as Rerck pulled Lenka's tongue out of her mouth without ripping it off. The major gently placed the cup and its saucer on the table and very deliberately began to open up the cut-throat razor.

'The Rogues are attempting to board the train,' shouted the radio operative seated by a desk in the middle of the room.

'Let them get aboard,' said the major, calmly. 'Then

147

give the signal for both Alpha Wolves squadrons to fall on them.' The major turned to the technician seated by the control panel. In a controlled and even voice, he gave an order: 'Begin'. The technician began flicking various switches and pushing numerous buttons that controlled the flow of oxygen and gas through the long yellow rubber tube attached to a combined extractor and pumping generator and a glass chamber positioned in the rear of Cerberus' carriage. He turned the large red dial, to *Gewinnen* (extraction) and placed his hand on the lever that would start the operation.

Next to the technician, in the corner by the rear door to the carriage was the glass chamber. Inside it were three more technicians, all wearing fully sealed body suits, sitting by another smaller, control panel with even more dials and gauges. The chamber was constructed to the major's precise specifications to ensure there were no leaks during the experiment. The three technicians began to blend the various gases that were destined to flood all four death wagons. Once the mixture was calibrated, these were fed into the yellow rubber tube.

The purpose of the instrumentation inside the glass capsule was primarily to adjust the mixture of gas fed into each of the four death wagons. Its secondary function was to record the time it took for the last occupant to die in each wagon. This was registered by the final scream or gasp coming from the speaker on the radio operative's desk which was connected to various microphones built into the roof of each of the four wagons. Thirdly, it controlled the ignition of the flame injectors based at the junctions of the copper pipes that ran along the walls of each wagon.

Finally, exactly five minutes after the jets of flame were extinguished, the plates in the floors of each wagon could be released to begin the distribution of ashes along the rail track.

Robotically, the three suited men in the glass chamber started to release various mixtures of cyanide, chorine and phosgene gas from the canisters positioned within their sealed glass chamber.

The technician outside the glass chamber lifted his hand up and pulled down the lever opening the main valve and activating the generator to begin the extraction of oxygen from all four sealed wagons. The three technicians turned to their uniformed colleague on the other side of the glass, nodded and smiled, now that the test of the death wagons was underway.

Lenka struggled violently against the reinforced leather straps that bound her wrists and ankles to the steel chair. But Rerck still held her tongue firmly in his fingers. She started to gag and then threw up over his boots.

'Turn the hose on her and your boots too,' ordered Cerberus with disgust. Rerck released her tongue as he undid the water pipe on the wall in case of fire.

'I am going to . . . to,' spluttered Lenka.

'Outside on the platform,' added the major.

Rerck dragged her, still bound to the steel chair, out to the platform between the carriage and the engine. Having cleaned his boots, he turned the hose on her. Flat on her back, still bound, she gagged on the water.

'Pig, free my hands or do you want to wipe me as well?'

Cerberus took another sip from his cup, as he shouted

to his bodyguard. 'It's a ploy to escape. Undo one hand, but keep hold of her throat. If she tries to free herself, snap her neck, but rip the tongue from her throat before throwing her from the train.'

Lenka looked dejectedly up at the man who grabbed her in his vice-like grip like a small injured bird caught in the jaws of a wild cat.

Inside the carriage Cerberus reclined in his armchair and looked away as Rerck unbound one of her hands. He wiped the froth from the corners of his mouth. After a matter of seconds he shouted. 'Enough! Bind her again and drag her in.'

Rerck did as he was ordered, nearly breaking her wrist in the process, before dragging her and the chair back into the carriage. Cerberus leaned out of his chair and stared at the choking woman, exposing the newly inserted teeth shaped to adapt to his shattered jaw.

'Your Englander has come to save you.' The skin below his right eye was now contracted to the extent that his eyeball looked likely to topple from its socket. 'The Irish are indeed as stupid as the British say they are.'

Chapter 14: Fierce Resistance

June, 1939 The Brandenburg Forest

Lenka looked out of the window and to her astonishment she saw Ryan swinging between the trees dangling from a rope. She looked at the major and his bodyguard, but neither had noticed the bizarre occurrence taking place outside.

Lenka's thoughts returned to those in the death wagons. There were no screams coming from the radio speaker: perhaps they were already dead.

The eyes of the technician standing beside her were fixed on the largest dial on the control panel. He shouted, 'Major, the de-oxygenation process is nearly complete.'

Cerberus looked up at the three technicians seated in the glass chamber, who were awaiting his order as keen as Pavlov's dogs. The major lightly dabbed the spittle from the corners of his disjointed mouth. He said in his sepulchral tone: 'Kill them all.'

Lenka continued to work the blade in her hand through the strap that bound her wrists.

The machine gunners situated on the open platform in the middle of the train turned the two *Maschinengewehr* (MG) 34 machine guns towards Ryan. The Irishman, who had been trying to avoid the tops of the trees, was now grateful that they were there as they absorbed the fierce automatic fire. The gunners took full advantage of the weapon's pivoting trigger design: switching from automatic fire to rip away the coverage provided by the dense forest, to semi-automatic fire when Ryan came into view.

Vodanski flew the gyrocopter over of the two MGs below, swinging Ryan up at a forty-five degree angle. The Russian then steadied the gyrocopter above the front engine.

Ryan untied the rope and dropped down onto the roof of the engine. He slipped on landing, but managed to grab hold of the steam pipe. It was so hot he immediately released it, but as he slid down the body of the engine he grabbed at and caught hold of one of the rigid metal fuel pipes.

Seeing that he could do nothing to help the Irishman, Vodanski fully opened the throttle of the gyrocopter and shot ahead.

Ryan dropped down onto the gangway that ran along the outside of the front engine. He was met by a Stormtrooper who lunged towards him. The Irishman launched his knife catching his attacker in the chest. As the man toppled from the train a second Stormtrooper ran onto the gangway. The Alpha Wolf stopped to open up with a *Maschinenpistole* (MP) 40 sub-machine gun, but not before Ryan shot him in the throat. The Irishman stepped over the body and made his way towards the front carriage – the same one he had tried to reach nearly a year ago before he was intercepted by

Grossmann, Cerberus' former bodyguard.

Jake drove the BMW R12 alongside the train riding at full pelt as the machine guns from the open platform in the centre of the train targeted their fire towards him. He managed to avoid the rain of bullets only by driving up onto the track. Bouncing violently on the sleepers, it took him four attempts before he could get close enough to launch himself onto the narrow step on the engine at the rear of the train.

A Stormtrooper, with a black iron mask covering his face apart from his eyes, was lying in wait with his finger on the trigger of an MP 40. But just as Jake hauled himself up on the gangway that ran along the length of the body of the engine, the train jerked violently. An unguided stream of lead ripped a clump of hair and skin off the American's scalp. Now lying flat on the platform, Jake plunged his US Marine Corps knife into the Alpha Wolf's boot. The man screamed before collapsing onto the steel platform, pulling back the trigger as he did so. As bullets clattered around him, Jake met the man as he fell with a blade under his jawbone.

Jake's world was now silent – the first blast from the MP 40 had removed his left ear, and the second burst shattered the eardrum in his right. Trying to focus, the American managed to lift himself up and made his way along the gangway of the rear engine towards the fourth death wagon. To his surprise two men train drivers ran onto the gangway and leapt over the rail. Both were immediately killed by the impact when they were met by Bavarian oak.

When he reached the death wagon the American shot the lock off the reinforced steel door and kicked it open. Inside the windowless wagon were women and children crying and frantically gesturing having been deprived of oxygen. Jake could not hear a sound. The American opened his arms, holding his palms downwards in an attempt to calm their fears. He began to lead them out and again with his hands he indicated that they should all crouch down in the rear engine of the train.

Jake noted that the twenty prisoners were evenly split between male and female and their ages ranged from infants to pensioners. He wondered if the make-up of the prisoners indicated some kind of macabre experiment, then he remembered who was behind it and knew for sure it did. As he continued to help the oldest and the youngest across the gangway, many opened their mouths but the American heard no words, some grabbed his hand to shake it and one elderly woman embraced him. Once all the living had crowded into the engine control room, he entered the pitch black wagon. There were three bodies, an old man and two children. He checked his ammunition cartridges and the grenades on his belt and wished he had more.

The American made his way to the end of the death wagon. Again he shot off the lock, but before he stepped onto the adjoining platform wooden chips flew up from the frame around the metal door. He jumped back as empty cartridge cases rained down from above.

Vodanski stood astride the wall of the bridge waiting for Cerberus' train to turn into the bend. It would have to slow down for him to have any chance of remaining on top of it when he jumped – having landed the gyrocopter in front of the arch of the tunnel below should ensure that it did. The Russian jammed the Tokarev TT-33 into his belt. He only had two clips, each containing eight cartridges, but he had selected the weapon because it could use 7.63 mm German ammunition – he knew he would secure an ample supply from the guards on the train that now cleared the bend.

The engineers at the front of the train watched firstly with fascination and then with horror, the fight between the two guards and the man who had landed on the roof above them. To their relief, having killed both Stormtroopers, the man disappeared. Only then did they turn around to look ahead, but again they could barely believe what they saw. The glare of the train's headlights reflected off the windscreen of an aircraft buckled-up on the tracks beneath the bridge ahead of them. Above it, was a huge man standing perfectly still on the wall.

Despite both drivers pressing down on the two brake levers, the train ploughed straight on under the stone arch, punching the aircraft through the tunnel and out into the open before it exploded. Debris scattered along the banks on either side. The engineers looked at each other in shock. Their arms were still locked on the brake levers, when they heard the radio operator's voice through the metal speaker above. 'Maximum speed. The major commands you to press on towards the Fortress.' The engine drivers exchanged glances, and then raised the levers opening up the valves to the engine – there was no debate as your fate could be decided by the slightest hesitation when the major gave you an order.

The gyrocopter had served its purpose. The impact had slowed down Cerberus' train long enough for Vodanski to leap onto it. But he did so only after the front engine, the carriage directly behind it and the first of the two black death wagons had passed beneath him. His target was the two MG 34s on the open platform situated in the middle of the train between the four death wagons.

The two pairs of machine gunners did not see or hear the Russian when he landed on the open platform in the space between them. They were focused on one thing, carrying out the prior instructions given to them by their commander. The major's orders were that if the train came under attack, they were to remove the machine guns from their fixed tripods and proceed through the four wagons killing everyone. Having detached the machine-gun, one of the Alpha Wolves heard someone behind running towards him.

Vodanski leapt into the air, landing with his knee in the base of a Stormtrooper's back shattering four vertebrae and snapping his spinal cord. The Russian turned to the other gunner and stabbed his knife down through the top of his skull.

Ryan lifted himself up onto the roof of Cerberus' carriage positioned in front of the four death wagons. He gripped onto the lip of the roof so he could ease himself down to a carriage window in search of Lenka. Suddenly, he caught sight of Vodanski in the distance standing on the bridge. Then, he caught a glimpse of where Vodanski had landed the gyrocopter. Ryan rolled back onto the roof of the carriage in the hope that by flattening himself firmly against it he would just about pass under the arch of the tunnel.

Ryan braced himself for the impact, but briefly opened his eyes to see Vodanski leap from the bridge. Immediately, it went dark and spears of flames began to shoot across his face. He kept his eyes firmly shut until the deafening sounds of the frenzied steel wheels disappeared, which told him that the locomotive had emerged from the tunnel. He flinched as his eyes were stung by the bright red glow of dusk.

Trying to regulate his breathing, Ryan rolled over onto his chest and began to lift himself up. Peering over the edge of the end of Cerberus' carriage he saw the leader of the Alpha Wolves for the first time since their encounter in Paris. The major stood with his back to him, on the platform at the back of his carriage. His arms were splayed out wide, as he repeatedly flapped his hands towards himself like a conductor summoning an orchestra to take their positions for the start of a performance. Ryan clenched his teeth as two trains appeared, powering at great speed on the new tracks on either side of Cerberus' train – the trap was shut.

Ryan took his Webley MK VI revolver from its holster to put a bullet in the back of the Nazi's head. Then he heard the familiar hysterical chattering of metal blades as insatiable steel teeth once again ripped through the black leather of his jacket into his back.

Three furious battles were taking place on Cerberus' train. Ryan was on top of Cerberus' carriage desperately trying to dodge each sweep of the chainsaw in Rerck's hands. Vodanski was on the open platform in the middle of the train battling the two masked Alpha Wolves trying to turn the MG 34 on him. At the rear of the train Jake was pinned down by a burst of gunfire directed by the Stormtrooper standing astride the roofs of the third and fourth death wagons.

The pincer attack that Cerberus had devised was in motion, as two heavily armoured trains, *Eisenbahnpanzerzüges*, emerged from the forest and closed in on Cerberus' train. Each of the newly constructed trains was identical to the one in the middle, except that on the central open platform in the middle of each was a Panzer IV tank with a 75 mm howitzer.

From the train to the right of Cerberus', Captain Ferranti was directing operations. Under his command in the carriages on each train were the remainder of the entire Alpha Wolves division. A radio operative sitting in front of Captain Ferranti delivered Cerberus' orders through the tannoys connected to the carriages of both advancing trains.

'Bewaffnen!' (arm) shouted Captain Ferranti, as the first of the carriages pulled parallel with that of Cerberus' train. The hundred or more Alpha Wolves on each train put on the iron masks that covered all but their eyes and engaged their MP 40s.

'Den Fuß aus Tür der nehmen!' (release the doors), as the hydraulic locks on the corners on one side of each carriage facing the train in the middle were detonated. The wooden doors of the eight carriages facing Cerberus' train shot into the air only to be crushed under the trains' impatient steel wheels.

'*Feuer!*' (fire), as a wave of rocket-propelled grappling hooks were launched from the encroaching trains across the roofs of the one hemmed between them. A second wave of steel bolts fired from crossbows followed, locking themselves to the four death wagons of the train in the middle, as if a hundred picadors had stabbed their lances into a bull. As more carriages from the two bordering trains were pulled alongside the central one, the Alpha Wolves lost no time in launching themselves across the gaps.

Lenka had nearly cut through one of the specially made reinforced straps that bound her to the steel chair. For the last few months she had experimented with how to hide the small, handle-less blade. When the Alpha Wolves finally ran down the stone stairs of the catacombs, she had opted to hide it inside her vagina wrapped completely in masking tape apart from two flat pieces of cork lightly taped on either side of the tip.

'Open all the valves,' ordered Cerberus. 'The gases must reach the wagons now; we shall waste no more time.'

The three technicians inside the glass chamber rotated all the dials to maximum.

Lenka continued to appear cowed while her hand worked the blade, which she managed to extract when Rerck freed her hand, feverishly into her bindings. Only the caged creature in the far corner continued to fix its empty black eyes on her in silence. Then to her surprise – as indeed it was to everyone in Cerberus' carriage – to her right a number of thick rubber pipes shot out from their moorings inside the glass chamber. Within seconds, the glass capsule was filled with gas. The three technicians inside began to gasp for air, ripping their white, sealed overalls to pieces as their skin blistered. Then with their fingernails they began ripping the flesh from their throats. Their faces mutilated into almost inhuman caricatures as their jaws dislocated, and their teeth shattered as they screamed. Cerberus and Rerck looked on expressionless – though Lenka saw that the major's right eye was bulging.

Lenka smiled. She understood the cause of the three men's demise – Jocky. The German engineers must have diligently followed the Scotsman's adjustment to the specifications in the original blueprint drawn up in the factory in Amsterdam. The Scotsman had deftly thickened the sketching of the cap inside the core inlet valve that was meant to fracture under the pressure of the gas. Now, as the pressure built up, it was the weaker rubber pipes connected to the control panel inside the glass chamber that ruptured.

The radio operative and the technician, on the outside of the glass capsule, were transfixed by the horror before them.

The major shouted an order to the technician who was standing by the control panel next to Lenka at the front of his carriage. 'Continue the operation. The glass is three inches thick. Cut off the gas and replace it with oxygen at full pressure until it does. Whatever is causing the blockage will fracture under the increasing pressure.'

The technician carried out the order without question and began to pump air back through the main yellow pipe.

'Any message from Captain Ferranti?' shouted the major at the radio operative.

The young man sat upright as if he had been slapped across the face.

'He reports that all Alphas on *Eisenbahnpanzerzüge 1* and *2* have engaged, but that they are meeting fierce resistance.'

Cerberus remained seated, twirling the ivory handled cut-throat razor slowly between his fingers. Seeing that the gas was contained within the chamber, he turned away. Through the window of the door at the rear of Cerberus' carriage the major watched the battles taking place, as the train continued weaving its way towards the Fortress, bringing each of the four death wagons in turn into view.

The major shouted to the radio operative. 'We cannot afford any survivors. Give the order for Captain Ferranti to turn the Panzers on the wagons.' The radio operator repeated the order to his counterpart in Ferranti's train. But, after doing so, he turned to his commander. He hesitated but thinking of the destruction that was about to be unleashed, he spoke. 'Major, could we,' he stuttered, 'could we not just stop the train until our troops overpower the enemy?'

Continuing to look out of the window, the major smiled. 'We are expected at the Fortress. I have promised Himmler that there will be no delay. This presents us with the perfect opportunity to test my *Eisenbahnpanzerzüges*.' Cerberus turned to the radio operator, his lips dripping with saliva. 'Your insubordination will be dealt with; whatever happens, you will not see morning.'

Cerberus' right eye widened a little as he examined the radio operator's flushed face.

'The pressure is dropping. The increased air pressure has released the blockage and oxygen is re-entering the sealed wagons,' shouted the technician.

'Can you bypass the system inside the glass chamber from the outside and release the gas directly into the sealed wagons?' replied Cerberus.

'Yes major, the gas canisters are already open. Their contents will simply drift through the network of pipes. It will take some time and I will not be able to monitor its effectiveness nor will I be able to adjust the blending, as the instrumentation is inside–,' He stopped, as he looked again at the faces of his three colleagues frozen in agony pressed against the glass partition.

'Do so,' ordered Cerberus.

Her hand was free. Now Lenka sliced the blade across the strap on her other hand and then into the ties that secured her ankles. The creature in the iron cage in the corner that had been panting, seemingly excited by her torture, continued to fix its cold eyes intently on her in silence. The technician turned when he heard the steel chair fall to the ground behind him and only got a brief glimpse of the short, handle-less blade before it severed his carotid artery.

The technician thrashed frantically around on the floor trying to stem the blood spurting from his neck, as Lenka began to slash at the hydraulic tubes that criss-crossed the control panel. Rerck ran at her, but she dived under his trunk of an arm as it swept towards her. She ran towards Cerberus. Before the blade in her hand could strike her captor, Rerck's hand seized her by the back of her neck as firmly as if it were the jaws of the savage beast in the cage. The gargantuan bodyguard threw her backwards, smashing her head into the desk. Rerck lunged at her, but before he was upon her, Lenka spun around and flicked the handle-less blade into the air. The blade disappeared into Rerck's left eye. The bodyguard screamed, but did not halt his advance. He launched his left boot into Lenka's chest. Lenka was again propelled into the air, landing against the wall of shelves stacked high with ledgers behind her.

'Restrain her but do not kill her,' ordered Cerberus calmly as he took a sip from the china cup. 'Yet.' He rose slowly from the mahogany chair, walked towards the desk and carefully placed the cup down beside the bone china tea set.

The major's right eye was so wide that it appeared that only his optic nerve held it in place. He looked down at Lenka's face pressed to the floor under Rerck's boot.

'Concealing a weapon in the one place that you knew I find too disgusting to touch. You duplicitous Jewish whore.' He licked the build-up of drool from the lopsided corners of his mouth, before he smiled. 'With the injuries we inflicted on you, it must have been incredibly painful to slip it inside you.'

Lenka swung her left leg at Rerck, but he grabbed it, lifted her up and yanked it violently, dislocating her left knee. She screamed as he dropped her to the floor. In agony, Lenka turned to look up at Cerberus.

'My vagina, along with the rest of me, healed some time ago. But you and this thick fucker were too dumb to realise it.' Rerck looked at his commander for instruction. Cerberus lifted his arm, indicating that he should stay his assault for now. The bodyguard lifted his hand up to halt the fast-flowing stream of blood from where he once had an eye.

'So you played the part of the helpless victim,' said

163

Cerberus. 'I surmise that even your Rogues didn't know that you had fully recovered.' He was now standing beside Rerck. 'So you were biding your time waiting until my Alpha Wolves seized you from the crypt, knowing that you would be brought to me. All those months wasted just so you could make one feeble attempt to kill me.' His right eye swelled as saliva continued to drip from his sloping lips. 'And you were willing to sacrifice a poor, young woman to do so.'

Lenka, said nothing, but it pained her that Bridgette was caught with her when Cerberus' men finally came to take her. After a brief struggle, Lenka hands were bound only for Rerck to force Bridgette down on her knees in front of her and snap her neck with one swift wrench of his hand.

'I take it you continued your sordid little affair with the Englander in the Catacombs.' He shook his head. 'I find it abhorrent that a gentile would mate with a Jew.'

Cerberus turned to look at the disabled control panel and then gave an order to the radio operator. 'Send a message to Captain Ferranti that I have need of his engineering skills.'

Cerberus peered down at Lenka and swept the side of ivory-handled cut-throat blade gently across her left cheek without adding to cuts on her face. He smiled. 'I see you have fire in your eyes.'

Jake could smell gas. He looked up at the broken feeder pipe above him, one of many that ran along the length of the ceiling of each of the four sealed wagons. The American traced it and saw that it was connected to a canister marked *propan gas* tucked under the lip of the roof outside the death wagon. He ripped it down. Jake looked again at the shadow on the connecting platform indicating the precise position of the man astride the death wagons above. He waited for the man to exhaust his weapon and reload, as he extracted his gun-metal Ronson cigarette lighter from his brown leather jacket. When the empty magazine of the MP 40 dropped down and bounced off the connecting platform, Jake made his move. He bent the pipe so it was outside the wagon and pointing upwards. He lit the stream of gas and jumped out of the wagon, as a fierce jet of flames engulfed the Alpha Wolf.

The American moved towards the third death wagon, not bothering to look at the screaming man burning to death who landed by his feet. Having kicked in the door of the death wagon, Jake was again met by the open, but silent mouths of the terrified occupants. It was the same mix of prisoners as in the previous death wagon, male and female and the young and old; only now they appeared to have a physical disability. He repeated the same gestures and helped to move them to the back of the train while trying to alleviate their fears – an impossible task, as they had to negotiate their way around the screaming man still writhing around in flames.

With all the adrenaline of the last few minutes, Jake only then noticed that he was bleeding heavily from wounds to his left thigh and shoulder. He pulled the bandana from his neck to tie it around the wide gash in his leg.

Now that he had evacuated everyone, he stumbled amongst the ghostly shadows of the death wagon. Five bodies lay on the floor, including a child whose legs were in calipers. Jake turned around to extract any weapons from the burning body, but it exploded before he reached it. The American regretted not trying to extract the grenades from the man's belt when he dropped down onto the gangway in flame.

Jake staggered to the door that led to the open platform in the middle of the train. He shot the lock off. As he kicked the door open, he jumped back into the wagon to avoid the expected spray of bullets from one of the MG 34s. Though all was silent, he could see the sparks as bullets ricocheted off the metal plates fixed to the inside of the sealed wagons.

Within seconds the rain of empty cartridges ceased. Jake dived out through the opened door, a revolver in each hand. The MG 34 to his left had the corpses of two Stormtroopers beside it. The other machine gun was raised in the air, releasing bursts of fire as Vodanski grappled with two Alphas who were trying to turn it on him.

Jake fired four times. The first two bullets hit each machine gunner in the neck: the paralysing shot. The following two entered one of the eye-sockets of each iron mask.

'Always late for the battle,' shouted Vodanski, expressing neither a welcome nor surprise.

The American saw the Russian's lips move, but taking an educated guess at the greeting offered he raised his middle finger in response.

A wave of steel bolts with ropes attached kicked up splinters as they punched into the wooden platform where Jake and Vodanski were standing.

Chapter 15: Black Cloth, Flesh and Bone

June, 1939 The Brandenburg Forest

Jake and Vodanski grabbed the two MG 34s. They remounted them on the tripods, gathered up the 900 round cartridge belts and slammed the stocks down, fixing them to the weapons. The Rogues immediately unleashed a torrent of fire at the Alpha Wolves swinging across onto the open platform. Those who managed to land on the edge of the platform were quickly dispatched by the merciless spray of automatic fire. Swarms of Alpha Wolves were cut to pieces. It was impossible to know how many for sure as bodies disappeared under the trains. There was no need for any exchange of words as the two Rogues synchronized their combat positions like they had many times before in the midst of battle, this time alternating their defence, one to machine gun their attackers while the other reloaded.

As Vodanski slapped in a third cartridge belt, he noticed the two crates positioned between the two machine gun posts. He ripped the lid off one. 'There is a God,' he shouted, as he gathered up one of the Model 24 *Stielhandgranate* stick grenades inside.

Jake did not hear the Russian shouting, but he realised what Vodanski had discovered when the first of the stick grenades whizzed past his ear. The American spun around, and when he saw the open box he kicked the lid off the other.

Again without a word exchanged, the Rogues adopted a new approach. When an Alpha Wolf appeared, he would be riddled with machine gun fire. Where there are no obvious targets, the Rogues would fix their guns on the windows of the carriages of the trains drawing alongside and, having shattered them, a grenade would follow.

The engines and front carriages of the trains on either side of Cerberus' train were ablaze. But despite this, the train to their right picked up speed and the Rogues then saw the greatest threat: the first of the black IV Panzer tanks. Painted in white along its turret was *Margarete 18* – the name of Himmler's wife and the year of her birth as Cerberus played to the Reichsführer's ego. It sailed past unperturbed as bullets from the MG 34s deflected of it like flies off a lion. Its turret now began to turn towards the second death wagon on Cerberus' train.

To their left, the other train also picked up speed. The second Panzer tank, again with markings painted along the side of the turret, this time *Lina 11* after Obergrüppenführer Heydrich's wife, came into view. It too was training its turret, this time on the third death wagon the one that Jake had liberated.

'Cover me you dumb Russian', shouted Jake, as he ignored the pain from his wounds and leapt across the gap towards *Margarete 18* with the machine gun. Vodanski stood up and rotated his bursts of fire so as to spray anyone who dared show themselves on either of the encroaching trains. As he did so Jake climbed the turret of *Margarete 18* and jammed the barrel of the MG 34 into the observation hole and began to empty its feeder belt.

The Russian lifted up the machine gun and trained its firepower on the rest of the train carrying *Margarete 18*. But, the turret beside Jake continued to rotate towards Cerberus' train and its revolutionary design of an extended high velocity 76 mm howitzer gun began to rip through the rear of the second death wagon as if it were made of papier-mâché.

Whatever carnage the American had inflicted inside *Margarete 18*, someone within managed to fire a shell. It whizzed past Vodanski and tore off one corner of the third death wagon before ripping apart the turret of *Lina 11* (an irony that was not lost on later historians as in reality the wives despised each other). The entire tank exploded, along with the ammunition boxes secured in the cages to its front and behind it on the platform.

Despite the burns to his face and right arm caused by the shell passing with inches of him and the metal fragments lacerating his face, Vodanski quickly got back on his feet. The Alpha Wolves that had taken cover on the train carrying what was now the blazing shell of *Lina 11* leapt towards Cerberus' train to escape the flames and the continuous explosions that tore through the carriages. Vodanski scrambled to the edge of the platform and released the full fury of the machine gun. Alpha Wolves were once again pummelled with machine gun fire. Those not cut to pieces by the MG 34 bounced off the walls of the death wagons to be pulverised by the frantic steel wheels below.

Jake began feeding the pineapple grenades from his belt through the just wide enough observer hole of *Margarete 18* – as if he were desperately trying to sate the appetite of the ravenous metal beast. Each time a pair of frightened eyes or fingers appeared on the other side of the aperture trying to block the grenades he would jam the barrel of the MG 34 into the hole and release a burst of fire. After he had fed seven grenades into the metal mouth of the tank, he pulled the pin on the eighth. After forcing it past the bloodied stump of a hand, he jumped down onto the platform and launched himself back across the gap between the trains still holding the MG 34 in both hands.

The roar that came from the destruction of *Margarete 18* was even greater than everything that had come from *Lina 11* – but Jake could hear nothing. As with their colleagues on the other train, Stormtroopers began to leap from the fires and explosions towards Cerberus' train. But now with the American's weapon accompanying the Russian's not one Alpha Wolf reached the train before being strafed by machine gun fire. Only the engine and the carriage to the rear of *Eisenbahnpanzerzüge 1* remained intact, while the engine of *Eisenbahnpanzerzüge 2* keeled over and plunged down the mountain side taking its burning carriages with it.

Vodanski was reloading for the sixth time, as Jake aimed his fire at the boxes of ammunition surrounding the burning shell of *Margarete 18*. More explosions followed, but despite this Vodanski heard someone jump down from the roof of the second death wagon behind him onto the platform. He spun around and saw an Alpha Wolf with the bloody fingers of his left hand missing, rising up behind Jake.

'Cowboy, behind you,' shouted the Russian. But the American didn't respond but continued to rain machine gun fire towards the other train. The Russian screamed again, but again Jake seemed to ignore him. Vodanski abandoned the cartridge-belt and leapt towards Jake. But before he reached Jake, the American's chest began to explode as the bullets from the Alpha Wolf's MP 40 punctured his heart and lungs. Jake dropped to his knees, as blood erupted from his mouth. He looked bewildered as Vodanski dived towards him.

The Russian knocked Jake onto his side, out of the Alpha Wolf's line of fire. But the Alpha Wolf threw himself down behind the critically wounded American. The Russian looked up from the floor as the man locked his damaged arm around Jake's face and slit his throat with his SS dagger with the other.

The Russian saw the grappling hook on the end of the rope that lay beside him. As he lifted himself up to assume a crouching position he grabbed it and hurled himself at the Alpha Wolf. One of the four spikes of the grappling hook went straight into the front of the stunned Stormtrooper's head, just above his iron mask. With the hook now locked on the man's metal face plate, Vodanski threw his feet up into the man's chest and launched himself backwards, keeping hold of the rope. Before the Russian landed on his back, the now taut rope wrenched off the Alpha Wolf's forehead exposing the cerebral cortex. If the man was not already dead, when Vodanski's sprung back up the follow-up punch he delivered to his exposed frontal lobe made sure of it.

Vodanski edged his way over to the American as machine gun fire rained down around him from what was left of the roofs of the death wagons on either side. When he reached Jake, the American lifted his hand and slowly removed a child's little white knitted hat from his sleeve. Jake's fingers froze, allowing the hat to rest in the pool of blood in the centre of his shredded ribcage: his eyes remained open but no longer moved.

Vodanski lifted the machine gun from Jake's hands, as two Alpha Wolves leapt down onto the platform. The MG 34 jammed, but the Russian grabbed Jake's knife from his belt and propelled it through the air hitting one of the Stormtroopers in the neck just beneath his iron mask.

The second attacker dropped down onto one knee to adopt a firing position. But before he could open fire, the Russian fell on him. Vodanski ripped one of the oval-shaped MG 39 grenades from the man's belt, and then the black iron plate off his face. Despite a furious struggle the powerful Russian smashed the grenade down into the Nazi's mouth. With the release pin end facing Vodanski, he delivered a right punch smashing it through the Alpha Wolf's teeth.

The Russian lifted the man up, pulled the pin still protruding from his bloodied mouth, and threw him from the train, sending him through the shattering window of the remaining carriage of *Eisenbahnpanzerzüge 1* which had drawn up alongside. Vodanski watched the horrified faces of the men looking out at him from the other windows of the carriage. The middle windows exploded and the ones still intact were bathed in red, like a drawn scarlet curtain dotted with fragments of black cloth, flesh and bone.

Vodanski heard screams coming from the ripped open roof of the death wagon ahead of him. He stamped his boot down onto the dead Stormtrooper's face to his right and wrenched the knife out of his skull. The Russian raised himself up to his full height and, despite his wounds, he advanced purposefully towards the cries coming from the damaged second death wagon.

Chapter 16: Rerck

June, 1939 The Brandenburg Forest

As frenzied metal teeth ripped fragments of black leather off his back, Ryan leapt from the roof of Cerberus' carriage. He landed face down on the roof of the first death wagon and above the din of the train and the clattering steel of the saw behind him, for the first time he heard terrified screams coming from below.

The cries were drowned out once more, as the sound of raging metal teeth grew louder. The Irishman flipped over onto his back. Ryan could now see Rerck, who had leapt from the roof of Cerberus' carriage and was standing above him holding a two-man chainsaw in his hands as if it were made of balsa wood. The black metal mask muffled his manic laughter – despite the handle-less blade embedded in the collapsed membrane of his eye hanging out of a socket of the iron mask.

Ryan lashed out with his boot, catching Rerck on the shin. Cerberus' bodyguard stumbled forward and fell on the chainsaw; its metal incisors once more tore into flesh.

At the front of the train, above him Cerberus had briefly caught sight of Ryan, followed by Rerck, leaping from his carriage to the roof of the first death wagon. But as they disappeared from view, he once again coldly observed the carnage taking place on the trains on either side before slipping back into his carriage. Without looking at the radio operative he asked, 'Any reply from Captain Ferranti?'

'*Eisenbahnpanzerzüge 1* is ablaze but it is pulling up alongside us, and he is boarding now,' replied the radio operative. The young man was trying to stay focused despite knowing that Cerberus would have him shot – if he was lucky – before morning.

Vodanski smashed the US Marine Corps knife down on the lock as he broke into the second death wagon. It didn't take much as the turret of the Panzer had ripped off most of the door frame above. He was met by a crescendo of coughing and crying, as the occupants desperately gulped in air flowing in from the hole in the roof.

Adults swept up children as they staggered or fell towards the open door. Unaware that part of the roof had been ripped open by the turret of a Panzer or that the door had been broken in at the other end of the wagon, two women continued to frantically stuff their coats into the nozzles of the extraction pipes. Between them, one man was still trying to leap up and seize a pipe to bend it down and close it – but Cerberus' design ensured that no desperate hand could ever secure a grip. With the light from the fires from the bordering train, Vodanski saw the horror of Cerberus' experiment. On the floor immediately below the network of pipes lay the bodies of eights adults who had tried to lift the children up to the roof in the hope of finding oxygen – an equal number of children lay silently beside them.

Now that the gnawing metal teeth were muffled by Rerck's

flesh and ribcage, Ryan again heard the cries from the wagon below. The Irishman dropped down onto the gangway connecting Cerberus' carriage to the first of the death wagons.

Ryan fired into the lock of the door of the death wagon. Though it broke the locking mechanism the door would not open. He put his right shoulder to it even though he knew the pain that followed would be as merciless as always. Such was his strength that he managed to force the door open by moving the pile of bodies behind it. He looked down at the faces frozen in horror. As oxygen filled the vacuum within the death wagon, Ryan heard cries and groans from within the pitch black darkness. He leapt over the bodies, ignoring the wrenching of the metal pins in his right thigh, as he released a number of rounds into the lock of the door at the far end of the wagon. Not waiting to see if it was no longer locked, he threw his right shoulder into it. The door broke away from the wagon taking the frame with it and allowing a gush of air to flood the death chamber.

Ryan turned around. Now, he could see bodies starting to stir. Some slowly made their way up onto their feet, others coughed and spluttered, but most did not move at all.

Having helped the ten survivors out of the second death wagon and directed them to head to the rear of the train, the Russian made his way past the pile of bodies. Before he reached the door at the front of the wagon, he heard a blast of machine gun fire before the door burst open. Vodanski emptied the last bullet in the chamber of the Tokarev into the throat of the man now standing in the doorway.

The second of the Alpha Wolves who had leapt from *Eisenbahnpanzerzüge 1* onto the gangway appeared behind his dying comrade. The Russian threw himself on him and grabbed the strap of his machine gun. Quickly, he wrapped it around the man's neck and started to throttle him. At seven feet, the Alpha Wolf was second only to Rerck in height in the elite unit. He struggled violently and managed to secure his hands around Vodanski's throat. But, such was the Russian's immense strength that the blood vessels in the Nazi's left eye began to burst, then his right. Vodanski then flung his right leg behind the man's right leg and swept it back, sending the blinded man backwards onto the floor. The Russian followed him down and locked him in a chokehold. Within seconds, all seven of the Alpha Wolf's cervical vertebrae shattered after Vodanski having repeatedly hammered his knee into the man's spine.

Ryan shot the lock off the front door of the second death wagon and kicked it open. Vodanski acknowledged the Irishman with one brief nod as he released his stranglehold on the Nazi, having broken his neck.

Ryan heard the roar of frantic metal teeth coming from behind Vodanski.

'Down!' shouted Ryan.

Vodanski immediately dived to the floor. Ryan dropped down on one knee to aim the revolver at the silhouette that now blocked out all but a few rays of light in the doorway opposite. But, as he took aim at Rerck he was seized by an iron chain around the neck wrenching him up into the air.

Chapter 17: Words Left Unspoken

June, 1939 The Fortress, Brandenburg Mountains

It was dusk, and a scorching red glow bathed the horizon.

With the chain he had thrown around Ryan's neck, Captain Ferranti dragged his captive into Cerberus' carriage. He tightened the chain just enough to make Ryan pass out, before looping it over the hook in the centre of the ceiling. The major raised his hand and the captain hauled Ryan up so the tips of his boots were only just touching the floor.

In the far corner of Cerberus' carriage, despite her dislocated knee, Lenka dragged herself over to the steel chair to lift herself up. As she did so, her eyes were fixed on Sean.

'We have much to do captain. Secure her,' said Cerberus.

Captain Ferranti, the recently appointed leader of the Alpha Wolves operating in fascist Italy and Spain, turned to the woman as he lifted the strap of the cross bow from his shoulder. He released the steel bolt from the weapon, hitting Lenka with such force that it propelled her back into another wall of ledgers that covered the wall. A number of ledgers toppled onto her from the shelves above, but not enough to smother her screams.

'Be respectful of my files, captain. The outcome of the war will depend on them,' snarled Cerberus.

Lenka continued to struggle, desperate to free herself from the bolt in her left thigh that pinned her to the wall.

Major Krak wiped the buildup of saliva covering his misshapen mouth. He did not look at Captain Ferranti who had turned away from the woman and once more stood to attention by his side.

'Reload and then hand me your crossbow, captain,' ordered his commander. The weapon in his hand, the major turned to the radio operator. 'Stand up'.

The young man rose unsteadily to his feet. His commander, with apparent disinterest, placed the point of the crossbow under his chin and released it. Cerberus turned away as the young man fell to the floor leaving a good ten feet between his body and the remnants of his skull and brain pinned to the roof. The major addressed Captain Ferranti.

'When the Englander regains consciousness, and for your sake, captain, he better, note the colour of his eyes when he locks them on me. Then when I give the order, secure his head in your hands,' he turned and smiled at Lenka, 'as I have work to do.'

Then when I give the order, lock his head in your hands.' He turned and smiled at Lenka, 'As I have work to do.'

Vodanski grabbed the loaded grappling hook and threw it the length of the wagon. It bounced off the wall, just missing Rerck, before the Russian charged at him. The one-eyed Nazi raised the chainsaw up to meet Vodanski. Before the frenzied steel teeth could tear into the Russian, he dived to his right. He landed on his knee and smashed his left elbow into the thick muscle in the back of Rerck's left thigh sending the gargantuan bodyguard to the floor. Rerck swung the chainsaw around as he fell, unleashing its gnashing teeth to feed on Vodanski's shoulder blade.

Undeterred by the blood and pain coming from his multiplying wounds, Vodanski delivered his clenched fist onto the flat edge of the knife sticking out of the Nazi's eye-socket. Rerck screamed, as the two huge men locked together in a stranglehold with the chainsaw tearing without prejudice into anything in its path. Vodanski wrapped his arms around Rerck's waist, while the bodyguard rained blows down on the Russian with his free hand. But though the bodyguard was a head taller and three stone heavier, Vodanski lifted him off the floor and ran him backwards into the metal plated wall of the wagon. Despite the impact, Rerck refused to release the chainsaw and drove it down on to Vodanski's back to feast once more.

Cerberus circled Ryan. 'Rerck discovered the chainsaw in the Church in Paris where you had used it to wipe out our French squadron. He has taken quite a liking to it as he has with the creature.' The major smiled at the beast, whose eyes were no longer locked on Lenka but on Ryan. Cerberus was having to dab the saliva from his thin lips as it was flowing freely as that from the jaws of the creature. 'As you have no doubt surmised from your wounds, he was eager to return it to you.'

He turned to Captain Ferranti. 'Where is Rerck?'

'He is dealing with the Russian in the wagon behind us.'

'Let's ensure he is victorious,' Cerberus said as he

looked towards the creature chained up and muzzled in the iron cage. Ferranti understood, though he was wary of approaching the creature. 'But first winch the Englander up to the roof.'

Captain Ferranti was eighteen stone, much of it muscle. Having hauled Ryan off the floor by the chain without the slightest change to his breathing he started to wrap thick leather material, reinforced with a steel gauze lining, around his arms. He slipped on a pair of the metal gauntlets and began to drag the cage containing the snarling beast towards the open door at the rear of the carriage. Though it was on runners, it took all the Captain's strength before he managed to drag the cage to the door. The Captain took the bolt cutter from the top of the cage. One of Cerberus' many mementoes – this was from his torture of General Vaux. He pushed it between the iron bars and began to cut through the muzzle that secured the creature's jaw. The beast remained perfectly still, biding its time. Before the harness hit the floor the creature smashed its foaming jaws through the bars at Ferranti. The Captain did his utmost not to show fear in front of his commander

With the carriage door open and the steel door of the cage now wedged into the doorframe, Captain Ferranti looked across at the two huge men were wrestling with the chainsaw between them in the first of the death wagons. Ferranti lifted up the steel door at the end of the cage, and the 95-pound beast leapt forward and disappeared into the open door of the death wagon. Quickly the captain pulled the empty cage back in just enough so he could slam the carriage door shut.

'Now use your engineering knowledge to repair the

severed pipes on the control panel,' ordered Cerberus. 'My guests must have made their way to the back of the train and I hope some have congregated in the rear wagon. We must not forget our core objective.'

Lenka threw her arm out to grab Ferranti's leg as he passed, but as he launched his boot towards her stomach. She curled up so it hit her in the chest causing her to throw up all over his expertly polished, though blood-splattered boots.

'Bitch!' shouted the captain.

'Fuck you,' she retorted as loud as she could.

The captain bent down and grabbed the woman by her hair. Seizing the end of the bolt, he ripped her thigh from the floor and dragged her over to the control panel. He smashed his boot down on the end of the bolt and again pinned Lenka firmly to the floor. As Lenka screamed, Cerberus nodded to the captain who began to reconnect the severed rubber tubes with masking tape.

Cerberus continued to slowly circle Ryan, as he slipped on his thin black leather gloves. The Irishman began to groan, despite the buildup of blood in his throat.

'Englander, you have performed an invaluable service. After each of our encounters, my superiors allocated more resources to me to ensure the inevitable destruction of the Rogues. Today is that day; you have served your purpose.'

Ryan lifted his head in search of Lenka. When he saw the mass of blood that covered her right leg, he clenched his teeth before turned to Cerberus. He was surprised that he was able to speak, but with his head up the blood congealed in his throat started to seep through the wound in his neck.

'I glad you feel . . . that blowing half your fucking face off . . . was worth it 'Crack'.'

His left eye began to bulge. 'It is pronouced Krak as in rake.'

'Crack . . . is more apt . . . as in arsehole,' spat Ryan.

'In Polish mythology the Krak dragon terrorised the land in search of human flesh.' The major seized Ryan's jaw in his elongated fingers. 'I would say that Krak is therefore the more apt, wouldn't you?' digging his fingernails tighter into the Irishman's jaw muscles so he could not answer.

Cerberus stared into Ryan's glacial-blue eyes. 'Of course you seek to distract me from the Jewish whore, but I am never diverted from my objective. Impulse, anger and desire, cloud the rational thought process.' He turned Ryan's face from side to side. 'At this moment I have but one thought, to hear your last breath.'

'You sick fu–' yelled Lenka, but before she could finish Captain Ferranti pressed down on the end of the steel spike with his boot. Satisfied upon hearing her screams, the captain continued to reattach the rubber tubes crisscrossing the face of the control panel.

Cerberus released his grip and continued to circle Ryan, while allowing the drool to drip freely from his chin. 'Nietzsche described joy as the feeling derived from when one's power is increased. If that is the case, then watching the increasing circle of blood forming below you is providing me with a sense of pleasure I could never have imagined.' He picked up a small glass container from the desk and opened it. 'I have had this for some time; it contains aspic. It was only after Paris I knew finally what it was meant to contain. I confess that the Jewess tested my patience earlier and I had thought of her tongue as a suitable object.'

Major Klaus Krak leaned in further towards Ryan's face. His right eye appeared to hang so far out of its socket that it was hard to discern what was keeping it in place. 'But of course once Captain Ferranti dragged you in here the final contents of the glass box were never in doubt.' Cerberus peered as if in a trance as he lifted a scalpel up to Ryan's eyes. 'I toyed with the idea of using the spoon I used on the Hungarian woman, but this is too delicate an operation.' His mouth opened wider, releasing a string of spittle, which began to coil up on the SS motif on his black collar. 'It will be a fascinating experiment, and I want to do all I can to ensure that the iris remains blue. I may even order our scientists to cut one open to identify what causes this abnormality. Perhaps they contain the essence of rage.'

Having repaired the connections on the control panel, Captain Ferranti turned towards his commander. 'All the pipes are reconnected.'

'Flood the wagons with gas and fire,' ordered Cerberus.

'Everything will be blown to pieces,' replied the captain, though he regretted his outburst immediately.

'You disappoint me, captain. Not a healthy position to be in. The gases, if you remember, are inert.'

'My apologies major. Of course, but what of Rerck?' asked the captain.

Cerberus ignored him. The captain pressed down on the main lever on the control panel that opened all the gas valves along the train and locked it into position. He lifted the four switches that were a secondary control releasing the gas from the propane cylinders and the ignition triggers that would propel flames through the sixteen jets in each death wagon. The two Nazis waited, but no screams were heard from the speaker on the desk.

'The Jewess must have damaged the fire propulsion system,' noted Captain Ferranti.

'Or my guests have departed,' said Cerberus.

'I'll finish the job Sean started on you, when I get up from here,' shouted Lenka. Ferranti kicked her once more, this time in the stomach. She threw up more violently and, barely conscious, rolled on her back towards the control panel.

Ryan pulled down on the chain. 'I'm going to rip your fucking heart out . . . and choke you with it.' The effort reopened the wound across his back, releasing a fresh stream of blood that disappeared into the crimson circle on the floor.

'If anyone is alive, we rely on the gas for now,' replied Cerberus. 'It looks like the Jew,' as Lenka's eyes closed, 'will cause us no further trouble until I can tend to her needs when we reach the Fortress,' said the major. He stood in front of Ryan and nodded to the captain to join him.

'Pull back the Englander's head', ordered Cerberus.

The captain grabbed Ryan's bloodied hair and wrenched his head back, exposing his neck. The major examined his souvenirs: various sizes of pliers, hammers, scalpels and saws. He selected the gleaming ivory-handled cut-throat razor.

'I swore, Englander, that if you ever fell under my hand again I would savour every moment and not let you die. Sadly, I have an appointment to keep and you are not invited. I will of course remove your eyes before your final breath, and have the knowledge that the last image you will ever see is me.' Cerberus slowly dug the blade into Ryan's neck and nicked his jugular vein.

As Cerberus extracted the blade and blood spurted over his face and jacket.

Lenka's eyes flickered open and then she screamed. 'Sean!'

Cerberus smiled as watched the blood stream down Ryan's body to the floor. 'This is not a comic book. In the real world heroes die.' The major continued to examine the incision like an artist admiring a brush stroke. 'A mortal wound, but just enough to make your death a slow one.'

Ferranti admired his commander's torture techniques and in particular his dispassionate execution of his victims, but for the first time he noticed that though he wore his thin leather gloves he was not wearing his customary apron. Nor did the major make any attempt to use his white linen handkerchief to wipe away the blood splattered over the black uniform.

'When I cut out his eyes, captain, wrench him right up to the ceiling and let the blood drain from him as one would a pig.'

The Irishman's crystal blue eyes remained fixed on Cerberus, as he tried to conserve what energy he had to free Lenka.

Lenka looked up at Sean's ashen face above his blood soaked body. She could do nothing, as she was still pinned to the floor. As hard as she tried, she could not free herself, and there was nothing near enough to use either for leverage or as a weapon. Lenka watched the blood drip faster into the large pool below the Irishman. She was determined not to cry, denying the Nazi the pleasure of seeing her tears, but the pain in her chest was as great as that caused by the bolt in her thigh.

Rerck's face was now a mass of pieces of flesh, blood and splinters of jawbone, as Vodanski knelt on his arms and continued to pound his fists into the iron mask. The lower half of Rerck's face, along with splinters of teeth, began to ooze through the small air holes in the iron mask covering his mouth like red-veined cheese through a grater.

The major's bodyguard still did not release the chainsaw in his hand. Instead, he waited for the opportunity to drive it back up into the body of the Russian.

An over-powering smell of a wild animal filled the death wagon. Vodanski remembered it from when he was a child, when the creatures' distinct scent sent villagers in panic to grab their children and run in terror to the nearest house.

The wolf leapt through the doorway, brushing past Vodanski who had flattened himself down on the casing of the chainsaw, causing Rerck to spew more blood across the steel-plated floor. As the creature tried to get traction when it landed, the Russian seized the animal by the fur on the back of its neck. He smashed it into the steel-panelled wall immediately above the men. With Vodanski distracted, Rerck seized the moment and swung the chainsaw up first into the Russian's stomach and continued upwards through his chest. As Vodanski's entrails spewed out over the Nazi, he seized the chainsaw and began to force it down and through the iron mask.

The Russian had intended to break the animal's neck against the steel wall, but such was its strength that it had bounced off and now fell on its master. The creature started to rip chunks of muscle from Rerck's neck, chest and arms, now rabid with the smell of fresh blood in its nostrils and the taste of warm flesh in its throat.

Vodanski fell back, throwing his arm across his body, but it made no difference as his chest was sliced open. The Russian placed his hand on his jacket to pull it across his torso to prolong his life if only for a few more minutes. The beast's head and fur were coated in blood as it swallowed Rerck's liver, but it turned and fixed its eyes on Vodanski.

The beast leapt into the air. But the Russian was prepared. He lifted his right arm to cover his throat – he had learnt from those that roamed his village as a boy that they always went for the neck first to paralyse their prey. The creature locked its fangs deep into Vodanski arm. As it did so, Vodanski lifted the beast into the air and swung his arm against the floor, smashing the jaw of the animal and driving the fragments into its skull.

Lenka looked up at Sean. His face was pale and drained of life: her man was going to die. The glass window at the rear of Cerberus' carriage shattered. The grappling hook that had caused it came to a stop a few inches ahead of Cerberus' face. But, only for the recoil to winch back sending one of its four prongs into Cerberus' right eye and another ripping open the right side of his mouth. Cerberus screamed before he was flung backwards into the air, landing heavily on his back on the floor by the open door at the rear of his carriage.

Ferranti ran past Ryan towards his commander. Ryan began to swing on the chain. Ferranti stared down at Cerberus. His commander's mouth was ripped open all the way to his right ear so that the muscle to his jaw was exposed and flapping on his bloody cheek.

The captain heard the swish of the chain behind him. Ferranti leapt up, spun around, only to be met by Ryan's boots smashing into his chest sending him crashing through the carriage window.

While hanging from the beam Ryan had managed to reduce the blood flowing from his throat by pressing his arms tightly to his neck. Supporting his weight by grasping the hook that held him, the Irishman lifted the chain over it and fell to the floor.

Ryan wrestled the chains from his wrists and grabbed the table cloth, sending the fine bone china tea set into the wall, before wrapping it around his neck. Totally disorientated, he turned his head in search of Lenka. Instead he saw Vodanski's body lying motionless on the connecting platform leading to Cerberus' carriage. In his hand was a grappling hook launcher.

With stunned incredulity Cerberus continued to stare over at Ryan from the floor.

Ryan staggered towards Lenka, only to collapse. Lenka finally managed to stretch her leg onto the control panel and use it as leverage to tear herself from the steel spike. She screamed as she ripped away part of the muscle from her thigh. Somehow she found the strength to turn over, raise herself up on her right leg and drag herself over to the Irishman.

When she reached him, she placed her hands gently on

his face. 'Our war is over, so don't die on me now Irishman.'

Sean looked up and coughed up a mouthful of blood. 'Drag me . . . to the engine.'

Lenka knew it was useless to argue, as the Irishman was as stubborn as she. She took Sean's left arm and began to drag him along the floor to the front of Cerberus' carriage. The major lay motionless on the floor, staring at Lenka as she grabbed the Webley lying on the desk and began to drag Sean across the floor. When she reached the door Lenka pressed down on the handle and pulled it open. Suddenly, Cerberus sliced the rope attached to the hook in his face with the ivory cut-throat razor. He leapt forward, darting across the bloody floor like a black salamander having finally selected its prey.

Cerberus' elongated, skeletal fingers reached up to seize her by the throat. She dropped the revolver and grabbed the hand holding the razor, but the other hand was now locked around her windpipe.

'Jew whore,' screamed the Nazi. Only then did he catch sight of the boot of the man who broke his jaw for a second time.

The Irishman lifted his boot again, this time smashing it into the apex of hook still embedded in Cerberus' face and pinning him to the door frame.

'You're going nowhere . . . Crack,' said Ryan, as his head fell back on the floor.

Lenka picked up the revolver and pressed it against Cerberus one eye.

Ryan lifted his hand. 'Leave him Lenka . . . he's as fucked as Hitler's barber . . . we . . . might as well . . . go to hell together.'

The two train drivers were shocked to discover the blood-soaked couple lying in the doorway behind them, with the woman pointing the barrel of Sean's revolver at each of them in turn.

'Full speed,' said Lenka. But both men, terrified from the carnage they had witnessed, did not exchange a glance as they both dived through the door to meet the same fate as their engineering colleagues at the other end of the train.

As Lenka dragged Sean into the engine cabin, two Stormtroopers leapt from the roof of Cerberus' carriage onto that of the engine.

Lenka swung Sean's Webley up and fired twice, but missed them.

'Why didn't they open fire?' But almost immediately, she understood why as a bolt burst through the roof and crunched into the metal panel in front of them.

'They must only have crossbows,' she said and looked down at Sean and pressed her hands against his cold and bloodied face.

A second bolt pierced the roof and struck the platform again only a few inches away.

Sean lifted his hand to rest it lightly on Lenka's face.

'Go . . . make sure that the families . . . are all in the last . . . wagon. Then . . . detach it . . . from the train.'

She bent her head down and pressed it against Sean's face.

'Stick to . . . our plan. Lead the survivors back to Berlin . . . and . . . and . . . to your friend Otto, the blind man . . . he will provide them with sanctuary.' Sean had to stop to cough up the blood in his throat. 'Then as soon as you have documents of . . . transit . . . take . . . take them to . . . the Rector in Paris.'

'We go together,' she pleaded, once again cradling his face in her hands.

He smiled up at her. 'Give me the gun . . . I'll . . . cover you . . . go.'

She held his blood-soaked face in her hands and kissed him. 'I–'

Sean put his bloody fingers up to her lips, 'Keep our secret safe'.

Lenka smiled before kissing him again, but as she pulled away his smile was gone and he just nodded making it clear that it was time to leave.

'The Alphas above us, I can–' she pleaded but this time he placed his fingers gently on her lower lip as he released two indiscriminate shots into the roof. She wanted to wrap herself around him and close her eyes for the last time, but she knew she had to lift herself up.

Slowly, she limped back into the carriage and stepped around Cerberus whose mouth was locked open by two grappling hooks' spikes embedded in the side of his head and nailed firmly to the doorframe. Only his one distended eye twitched frantically, like that of a chameleon caught in a cloud of flies.

Lenka turned to look at Sean. To her surprise he winked and smiled as she turned away from him for the last time.

As she made her way through Cerberus' carriage, ahead of her in the doorway at the far end, lay Vodanski's body. Beside him was the blood-soaked carcass of the dead wolf: no longer salivating as it had been as it watched her torture. To the left of them was the barely recognisable half-eaten corpse of Rerck. Knowing it was futile, she gingerly bent down and pressed her fingers to the right side of Vodanski neck in search of a pulse. There were none, but she let it rest there for a few more seconds. Lenka noticed the bloodied little white hat sticking out of Vodanski's jacket. She lifted it out, raised herself up and limped unsteadily towards the second death wagon. As she entered, she saw Jake's body lying still on the open platform ahead.

Having reached the end of the wagon she knelt down once more on her right knee, beside Jake. She placed her hand on the small section of his blond hair that was not soaked in blood. She looked again at the little white hat in her hand and pieced together the events that led to it leaving Jake's sleeve – where he thought it was hidden from all – to it being in Vodanski's coat.

Ryan crawled towards the controls, leaving on the floor the revolver he could no longer lift. Another steel-tipped bolt burst through the roof and landed in the centre of the floor slicing his cheek an inch below his scar. Ryan looked up at the darting eyes peering through the holes in the roof desperately searching for him. Another bolt kicked up splinters by his face as he continued to drag himself towards the controls. Two more steel bolts tore through the roof; the first shattered Ryan's left shoulder and the second broke his right hip. Ryan could barely breathe as a third steel bolt shattered his left ankle. He had so little blood left that he barely felt the pain coming from his latest wounds. Where his body was not cold, it was numb.

The train powered on. They could not be far from the Fortress, so perhaps the plan he and Lenka had hatched in Paris would work after all. Ryan rested his bloodied face against the floor. He thought of Chris' last words, 'It's time', and closed his eyes.

'Sean! I've uncoupled the rear wagon and the engine, but we are still stuck to the train as it's slowed down. We need you to pull away!' came Lenka's faint voice from the radio station in Cerberus' carriage. He had no idea how long he had been unconscious, but was amazed he was still alive

Ryan could hear gunfire coming from further down the train.

'Help us Sean!' Lenka's voice was barely audible now.

Ryan lifted his head and pressed himself against the floor with all the strength he had. At the fourth attempt the bolt in his shoulder came away from the wooden floor, followed by the one through his hip. He bent his knee sharply, tearing a chunk of flesh and bone away from his foot while the bolt remained embedded in the floor. He once again began to drag himself across the floor. Another bolt smashed into his left femur and again he ripped his body from it.

He lifted himself up the engine panel with his right arm; the metal pins in his body were no longer angry with him now that a cold numbness encapsulated his body. Ryan threw his hand up onto the lever and pulled it down, opening the valve and pumping oxygen into the furnace. Slowly, the rhythm of the steel wheels turning grew louder, as the flames from the furnace whipped the train into a fury.

As if he had been shaken from a state of shock, Cerberus realised that the train was once again racing towards the Fortress at full speed.

'You'll kill us,' he yelled as he tried and again failed to wrench his head away from the hooks nailing it to the doorframe. 'It won't make any difference if you destroy the Fortress. The Reich will build more,' he screamed.

'Oh . . . I'm sure you psychos will build . . . more,' said Ryan tried to regulate his breathing as he had one final surprise for the Nazi. 'But don't hold your hopes up that the next lunatic . . . who steps into your shoes . . . can rebuild the Fortress.'

Cerberus' right eye began to open and bulge once more.

'You're a fool Englander if you think my train will level the Fortress. Our scientists modified the gases; all are inert.'

'I knew this Scotsman . . . you met him once. A funny little fellow,' Ryan gasped, as blood continued to clog in his throat. 'He was always tinkering with things . . . and . . . not just the mechanics.' Ryan's head dropped as more blood streamed relentlessly through his fingers clasped to the wound in his throat. 'He was also a half-arsed . . . chemist. In Amsterdam he told me he tweaked the designs so that your robots . . . would construct each pump with a reservoir . . . ten times its original size. . . all containing ethanol . . . he knew a bit about alcohol my friend.'

Cerberus could only move his mouth now. 'A cleaning solvent, what harm can-'

'My little friend said he got the idea from your scientists . . . who are experimenting with ethanol . . . to use

196

as rocket fuel . . . He said that when ignited' – Jocky had added, "you have a gift for that kind of thing Irishman" – 'the Nazis might be the first to reach the Moon.' Ryan rested his head back against the panel as there was no longer enough blood to lodge in his throat. 'Thanks to your train . . . when we race into the Fortress . . . everything . . . including your files   . . . will all be blown to . . . bol . . l.ocks!'

Cerberus could only move his mouth now. 'A cleaning solvent, as long as it's contained-'

'My little friend adapted the design of some the valves . . . so they drain the reservoirs . . . pumping the ethanol through the train. . . They say you can use it . . . as rocket fuel . . . Thanks to your help, when we race into the Fortress, everything . . . including files . . . on enemies of the Reich . . . will be blown to . . . bollocks!'

For the first time in his life, Cerberus realised that it was he who had been manipulated. 'My ledgers!'

There was no media coverage of the explosion that reduced Himmler's Fortress to rubble. However, local villagers reported that when the train pounded under the main arch it was travelling at such a speed that no one could have survived. Meanwhile some four kilometres away the party that the Führer was due to attend the following day to celebrate the first anniversary of the Munich Agreement was cancelled. The official statement was that the Chancellor had some important matters of state to attend to. No mention was made of the urgent requirement to replace all the windows.

Chapter 18: A Wisp of a Girl

September 1939, London

'Miss Lenka Habermann, it is indeed a pleasure to finally meet you,' said Winston Churchill, as he ushered the woman into his Parliamentary chambers. 'Who would have thought that your letters to me all those years ago asking for some books, would lead us here?'

'Thank you for all your kindness to the orphanage,' said Lenka, but she did not accept the Statesman's offer to sit down, preferring to support her weight on her cane. 'What of the children?'

Churchill did not sit down. 'The families you saved from the train have been relocated across the country. Those children still recovering are receiving good care in Great Ormond Street Hospital, a few miles from here. They are doing well, but many were in a terrible state even though your friends in Paris did an excellent job caring for them. I have been told that when they arrived, they were well fed, clean and had been provided with fine new clothing.'

'Do you expect any international action after what the Nazis did to them?'

Churchill smiled. Now that he had finally met her, the fortitude of the woman that stressed every stroke in her letters was inescapable – she never lost sight of the enemy.

'I fear not. We have no evidence beyond the fact that

the Nazis were transporting a number of families of supposedly known "state provocateurs" to a secure facility. When British officials challenged the German Ambassador about the existence of death wagons, the official response was that a mechanical failure on the train led to a number of chemical leaks. Both governments have agreed that the matter is closed as there were no recorded passenger fatalities.'

'What of the four children that the Rogues rescued from the hospital on Lake Como? Sean's sister has allowed a British doctor access to them. Was there any evidence of what the Nazis did to them?'

'Tests confirm that they were injected with various chemicals, but our doctors have been unable to ascertain which ones. We do know that no painkillers were administered. As for witnesses, all the Rogues that were there are now sadly dead.'

'And nothing else?'

'As Ryan once told me, the man who led the Alpha Wolves was an expert at eradicating any evidence that would implicate his superiors.'

Lenka had no doubt that the man she had been in correspondence with since she was a child was as dejected as she. 'I'm the last of the Rogues and as you can see, I am hardly a threat to the Nazis. Your voice is all that remains now, while my country prepares itself for the worst.'

'Following the Nazis invasion of Czechoslovakia I implored the Government to declare "thus far, and no farther". It is only through perseverance that man has learnt to stand upright, instead of walking on all fours. I have no doubt that the British people will confront the threat the

Nazis pose to our liberty; however, by then I fear that it may be too late for your homeland.'

Lenka handed the Mauser over to Churchill. 'Sean said to say thank you for the loan but it kicks like a mule and it should only be used to stop papers blowing away.'

Then she handed him a package tied roughly with twine, whose contents also contained a note from Sean with an address.

Churchill looked down at the weapon that he had entrusted to one other man. He smiled, but it disappeared when he lifted his head.

'The Irishman believed there was a traitor on our side.' Lenka said nothing. 'There are those with fascist sympathies,' – Lord Sloane came to mind – 'particularly in higher circles, who are enamoured of the Narzees. Many are just bungling idiots, but this does not make them spies. However, if we find that any of our people are in league with the Hun, they will be hung for treason.' He paused and smiled. 'You remind me of Ryan as you say so much, when you say nothing.' Lenka returned the smile. 'I take it the matter is being dealt with.'

Lenka turned to go.

Churchill was not by nature interested in private affairs, unless they were those of a friend.

'Did you care for the Irishman?'

Lenka turned to the man standing in the centre of the room, who had struck a match to light the cigar he lifted from the box on the desk.

'I loved him,' she said and then closed the door.

Minutes later, Kathleen, Churchill's personal secretary,

entered the room.

'Sir, the journalist from *The New Statesman* has telephoned to ask if his interview with you this morning can be moved to lunchtime.'

'Is that the publication that in 1926 asked the question, "Should we hang Mr Churchill or not?"'

'I'm not sure, Sir.'

'I am.' He took a draw on his first cigar of the day. 'Hmmm, the conclusion was that on balance I should be hanged to be on the safe side.' Churchill smiled like a mischievous child. 'Good, tell him the interview will be at midday, providing he is not erecting my gallows at the main gate. Also, find out if he enjoys good malt.'

'I fear the interview will not be kind. Your criticism of the Government only increases your unpopularity with the Press.'

'Criticism is never agreeable, but it is necessary. It fulfils the same function as pain in the human body; it calls attention to the development of an unhealthy state of events. If heeded in time the danger may be averted; if it is suppressed, a fatal distemper may develop.'

Kathleen returned to her office and telephoned to confirm the meeting with the journalist and returned to Churchill's chambers two minutes later. She was diligent, but saw no need for small talk with any journalist about to besmirch her employer.

'Sit down,' the Statesman said as he poured and handed her a glass of *Glenfiddich*. 'Or would you prefer a flute of *Pol Roger*?'

'I'm not one for drinking.'

'A failing I will not hold against you,' he said as he

handed her a tumbler containing two fingers of whiskey.

In all her time in his employment he had never invited her to share a drink with him.

'The war will begin soon,' Churchill said as he slumped into the red leather armchair.

'We will be ready.'

'Will we?' Churchill thought for a moment. 'Good, that's the spirit that will crush the Narzees.'

'Forgive me for asking, but is something troubling you? Would you like me to contact your wife or the Admiralty?'

'No.'

'Is it to do with that wisp of a girl that was here?'

Churchill beamed a cherub-like smile. *A wisp of a girl; if only she knew*, he thought. 'Yes, and her friends.' He took a sip from the glass. 'Remember the Irishman?

'Yes.'

'Well, that wisp of a girl, the Irishman and a few others, have been standing alone against the Narzees for over two years. A little war that perhaps no one will ever hear tell of.'

'A guerrilla war.'

'No, that would do them an injustice. They fought only to save lives. By default this kept the Germans busy, diverting their best fighters and resources away from the frontline.'

She knew the Statesman was grandstanding, talking as if he had the ear of the House, but she knew that such was his way.

'Of course they couldn't defeat Germany, but that was never their goal. Their fight was for our humanity, for common decency, to challenge the beast within us and remind us what it is to be human.'

'Apart from the girl, are any of them alive?'

The Statesman responded with a slow shake of his head.

'Sir, was it was worth their lives?'

'Liberty always comes at a price, and they paid for it with their lives. They would have said it was worth it, as they risked their lives to save a number of children: and thankfully they succeeded in their mission.' He spoke now only to himself, 'Providing we learn from it and do not forget.'

Kathleen felt compelled to break his sombre mood.

'Then it was worth it, as we will not forget.'

It had the desired effect. Churchill nodded. 'During The Great War many German troops committed crimes against the civilian population because they said they were ordered to – as if this negated their responsibility to the rule of law and humanity. The men and women who called themselves Rogues would I know refuse such an order. As war clouds gather once more over Europe, let us not descend into barbarism: that is the legacy of the Rogues.'

He brightened up as he looked at Kathleen. 'Many say I am alone, but I am not. War is horrible, but slavery is worse, and you may be sure that the British people too would rather go down fighting than live in servitude.'

Kathleen knew that the Statesman wished to be left to his thoughts. She got up leaving her drink untouched, while Churchill walked to the window that overlooked the Thames. He opened Sean's parcel. He extracted the note and nodded as he read it.

'Sorry Sir, is there something else?'

'Yes, a request from the Irishman. There is a little girl who is mentally impaired, called Elizabeth Penhaligon. He wanted us to find a good home that will be suitable for her needs. Also, to give her this.'

Kathleen was surprised to be handed a recently washed and re-stitched rusty-coloured teddy bear. 'Is the girl a relative of his?'

'No, she is the daughter of a dead British serviceman who I know to have been an old enemy of his.' Churchill examined the puzzled look on Kathleen's face. 'He was a very complex man, the Irishman.'

'You respected his stand against Nazis, but was the Irishman a good man?'

'A good man? No, not in the sense that society or the Establishment would judge him so. He was a man who killed many but who also witnessed man at his most barbaric, yet he refused to be brutalised by it. My opinion, for what it is worth, is that he was not what I would call a good man but rather a man who was true to his beliefs.'

Kathleen was about to leave but watched as the cigar smoke began to cloud the red glare of sunset. For the sake of his family she hoped that the interviewer would be a little kinder with his pen this time.

The Statesman stared unseeingly out of the window; his thoughts were not of journalists but of dictators.

Chapter 19: Lord Sloane's Secret

September 1939, London

Lord Sloane entered his office in the Admiralty Building. He was startled to find a slightly framed woman sitting in his huge black leather armchair. She reminded him of an illustration in a children's book he once flipped through of a child who had jumped onto the King's throne out of mischief. He bought the book, but never sent it to his daughter.

Lord Sloane closed the door. 'You must be Lenka,' he said as he turned, pointing his Browning revolver directly at her. 'State your business or I'll shoot you on the pretence that you are a burglar.'

'Sean wanted you to have this,' Lenka replied. As she slipped her hand into her right-hand pocket, Lord Sloane cocked the trigger. Lenka removed a gold pendant and chain. 'This is yours.'

He recognised it and slowly lowered his gun. Lenka used her cane to ease herself up and walked towards him from behind the table. She was just over half his height when she stood in front of him. 'Your daughter gave it to her husband. He in turn passed it to Sean as it contains a photo of his daughter who the Nazis held as a hostage.'

The aristocrat said nothing. He was transfixed not by the locket that he had last seen nearly thirty years ago, but by the family photo inside it.

Lenka looked up at the man. 'You were on a reconnaissance operation in the Balkans before the First World War. I guess you met her mother there.'

Her eyes remained fixed on the man. 'At least you gave her more than a baby before you fucked off.' Lenka continued to make her way slowly to the door with the aid of her cane.

The aristocrat hesitated, but in a quiet and controlled voice he asked, 'How did you know Magdalena was my daughter?' Lenka was surprised that he did not deny it; in fact, there was resignation, even sadness in his voice.

'Sean read the inscription on the back. It was inscribed "*Virtutis Fortuna Comes*" (Fortune Favours the Brave): it is the motto of The Duke of Wellington's Regiment: your regiment.'

The man still did not look at Lenka but stared at the pendant in the palm of his hand. 'I was a young man, just married. I couldn't afford the scandal.' Lenka turned from him and hobbled to the door. 'It was the Americans who first came to me with the names of Magdalena and Tóth. I could not get involved, but instead I suggested they approach Winston. I knew he would care little for the risk to his position or reputation and would do all he could to help them.'

'Then you pretended to confront Churchill at his home, but stated that there was little you could do to stop him. Churchill knew you were manipulating him as he said you overplayed your hand. As he put it, quoting Shakespeare, "The Lord (rather than lady) doth protest too much".'

'I needed to keep as much distance as I could from

Magdalena. I had too much to lose. The plan would have worked, but they were betrayed.' He paused solemnly then lifted his head up to look at Lenka. 'Do you know who the traitor is?'

'Yes.'

Lord Sloane slipped the locket and chain into his pocket.

'I still believe that Winston is wrong about the Nazis; we can make peace with Germany. It's not too late.'

She did not look back as she said before slamming the door, 'The Nazis tease fools, like cats toy with mice.'

Chapter 20: Amelia's Story

October 1930, Cheltenham

Amelia was raised in the knowledge that she was privileged, and it was something that she was entitled to rather than be humble about. Her family had a stately home in Berkshire, and she had the finest clothes, handmade to her personal requirements, a most exclusive education and the most delightful holidays in Europe. There was nothing she could want that she did not already have. But with the global turmoil that followed The Great War, she and her circle had one fear – that they might lose it all.

Her father was a millionaire having made his money from numerous trading ventures secured through his social circle across the Empire and was so well connected that Amelia and her sisters would run around at garden parties in the Palace. This was after the turn of the new century, and much had changed in the world. First there was the Russian Revolution and then the Great Depression. Now workers, even the family's servants, were heard to question their place in the established order. To Amelia and her family, this posed a direct threat.

Beneath the family hauteur lay a hatred of Jews. Anti-Semitism was engrained in many societies, irrespective of wealth, and rarely tempered by education.

It was not rational or to Amelia's knowledge

influenced by any immediate experience of Jewish people, but instilled in them down through the generations. Her parents, her friends, many of aristocratic blood, and all of the public school system saw Britain becoming a Jewish-dominated country. On his death bed, Lord Arbuthnot Brett, her grandfather, raged at the indignity of having Benjamin Disraeli, born a Jew but who rejected it, as prime minster.

In the Brett family home, a grand twenty-bedroom mansion, lay a further insecurity, a distrust of the democratic system. It was a fear rarely voiced, except in the late hours amongst their social circle when brandy had loosened tongues. Democracy offered the opportunity for socialists to enter government. There was also talk of the provision of universal higher education. The 'establishment' faced the frightening prospect that positions of authority might be awarded on merit.

In her first year at Cambridge studying French and German, Amelia found herself mixing for the first time with those from a working class background – not many but enough to ruin her time there. She had nothing to say to them and, in truth, she saw no reason to. What was frightening was that many students, usually from the upper-middle classes, spouted left-wing slogans about worker's rights; some even declared themselves communists.

Her course took her to study in Munich for a year, having rejected an offer from the Sorbonne. It was an exciting period for the young woman. The Government of the Weimar Republic stated it had no sympathy with the German Communist radicals, but years earlier it had been Adolf Hitler's *Schutzstaffel* (SS) and Ernst Röhm's

Sturmabteilung (SA) that chased the radicals from the streets. Now Hitler was chancellor and all dissent was ruthlessly suppressed for the good of Germany. Here was order – and Amelia was excited by it. She was enthralled by the specacle of it all – her heart pounded as striking, deadly black uniforms marched to the stomping of leather boots arrogantly descending on cobblestones. She would run along with the German students after classes to experience the euphoria of Hitler's rallies. Soon she became an active participant. She gave up her annual holidays to St Tropez, instead opting to join the invigorating experience of Nazis gathering in Odeonsplatz each weekend followed by one beer with the Stormtroopers in the Englischer Garten.

One Sunday afternoon, she took tea with an officer in the SS. He was tall and his facial features looked as if they had been sculpted from white marble. With his sun-bleached hair he was the epitome of Nietzsche's Superman. She stayed with him all afternoon, as he posed in a fashionable studio for sketches commissioned by Goebbels for the cover of the Nazi newspaper *Völkischer Beobachter*. His only visible flaw was a scar over his left eye, but this only added to his attraction, giving the impression of a man of action.

As he walked her home, she confessed her uneasiness at the term Socialism in the name of the Nazi party. The officer quickly dismissed her concerns by assuring her that the name was purely to attract the German worker to the movement. 'All armies need fodder,' he laughed, exposing the perfect alignment of bleached white teeth. He explained to the captivated young British woman that the established order in Germany, and all other countries ruled by the

Nazis, would remain as it was now. As they turned into Marienplatz, a group of SA were beating up a man who did not have the correct papers – ones with a German surname. The man and his family had that morning been forcibly ejected from their home, so that a German family could take control of all they possessed except for the clothing they could carry.

'How terrible,' said Amelia to the dashing officer, but he quickly alleviated her fears.

'They are Jews.'

Her mood changed abruptly. 'They bring it upon themselves. My mother told me that Stalin is Jewish,' she said as she clutched the officer's arm a little tighter.

She thought no more of the incident. On the doorsteps of the house that her father had rented solely for her, the officer kissed her hand but did not release it. As he lifted his head, she looked up at him. 'I wish Britain had someone of the calibre of Hitler or Mussolini who would bring order. All this sabre rattling by Churchill and his ilk is ridiculous. Our countries are natural allies, and we should be fighting the Communists together.'

'You are right, Frauline Brett. Germany has its territories as does England. Our racial superiority gives us the right to subjugate all others.' He grinned. 'We even share the same Royal family.'

The officer was pleased to see that her frustration had turned to anger.

'My father has often said that The Great War was a ghastly mistake.'

The officer's smile broadened as he took her other hand in his. 'Perhaps together we can bring Britain to its senses.'

She squeezed his hands tightly and almost standing at attention replied, 'Yes, if there is anything I can do.'

'I will have a word with my commander; perhaps he can think of a way.'

Ten minutes later the officer entered the Brown House, as it was known, the headquarters of the National Socialist Party on Brienner Straße. He smiled at the receptionist as he presented her with an open rose. She held it to her nose and smiled. 'Gretchen, please tell Grüppenführer Heydrich that Oberleutnant Brunner is here to file his report on the British aristocrat.'

Chapter 21: The Scent of the Bitch

September 1939, London

The darkest of sunsets cloaked London as if it were veiled in the finest of crimson silks. Lenka stood in a doorway opposite the big white Georgian house in Berkeley Square. As she waited to enter the woman's house, it brought back memories of their first meeting when all the Rogues gathered together in the underground bar in Berlin. Now, she was the last of the Rogues.

Ten minutes later, after the last of the servants had left, Lenka was at the back of the building she had kept under surveillance for the last four hours. She wrapped her hand in her scarf and punched it through the glass pane of a kitchen door. She put her hand through the hole in the glass and turned the doorknob. Her progress was slow but she had the aid of a cane, and she was in no hurry.

She made her way into the drawing room. The walls were decorated with red silk wallpaper; higher still were gilt-plated plaster moulds that buttressed the walls to the ceilings. The carpets were of the thick Persian kind. The focal point of the room was the Murano glass chandelier, suspended from a four-foot wide rose cornice, constructed of daggers of real crystal that would not be out of place in the finest of palaces. Lenka knew nothing of the origins of the numerous carvings and statutes, the furnishings or the history of the house; she only knew that it was as alien to her as lipstick to her lips. She poured herself a brandy, drew the curtains and sat in an armchair in the far corner of the front room.

An hour later the key turned in the front door. Lieutenant Amelia Brett turned on the light in the dining room and discovered the person she despised more than any other. 'How did you get in?' she demanded. Lenka ignored the question. 'I'm calling the police.'

'The line's cut. You could try to shout out of the window,' as she spoke, Amelia could see the gun in the woman's hand. Lenka indicated with the movement of the barrel of Sean's Welrod 'suppressor' that the English woman should sit on the armchair opposite with less than a metre between them.

'Is Sean dead?' asked Amelia, as she smoothed her skirt before she sat down.

'Yes.'

'Why are you here?'

'Because of Sean.'

'I don't see–'

'You betrayed us.'

Amelia was shocked and when she finally was able to speak, she protested her innocence. 'I risked my life to help all of you.'

'After we met you that first time in Berlin, Sean checked your background. You didn't just study German; you lived there for a year.'

'I don't tell my business to the likes of you people,' spat the lieutenant.

Lenka raised her eyebrows and smiled. 'Every piece of

information you gave us led us into a trap. At first Sean thought it was your plan to give him the names of Magdalena and her son, to use him to find them as your Gestapo friends couldn't. He also thought you might be using him to draw anyone else like him out into the open. But later, having escaped the trap set at Budapest Station, he realised that he was the target.'

'This is nonsense.'

'It was you who put Sean's name forward for the operation.'

The lieutenant shook her head. 'You're mad; what proof do you have?'

'You were the liaison officer for the Admiralty, so you knew of Lord Sloane's entreaties to save the woman and the boy. I bet you couldn't believe your luck when he covertly engaged the support of Winston Churchill. Was it you who organized the dossier on Sean to be sent to him?'

'Why would I do that?'

Your bosses in Berlin wanted vengeance after Sean disrupted a number of their Italian allies' activities in Ethiopia and later their own in Norway.'

'Your brain is addled. You and your Rogues have a propensity to drink hard.'

'When Sean escaped assassination in Bulgaria, you enacted a new plan, one that would strengthen your links in the British Secret Service.'

'You are insane.'

'You knew that there were those in the British Secret Service who wanted Sean dead for his involvement in Bloody Sunday and the death of a number of their colleagues. You probably thought how grateful they would be, if you enlisted their help in having the IRA kill him in London. Having played such a prominent role in the death of Sean, young men in the British Secret Service would wink at you as they passed you the secret files you requested for years to come.'

'Are you mad? All this just to kill one dysfunctional, Irish lunatic?'

'No, you had a far greater target. If Sean had been assassinated in Budapest, your Nazi bosses would have released the details of Churchill's role, along with that of Sean's in the Irish Civil War. Churchill's few political allies would be appalled. His disgrace would be even greater than that he suffered after the debacle of the Dardanelles. Your most vocal opponent would finally be silenced.'

'So now all this was to remove one already isolated old man out of the way?'

'Sean believes that there was another facet to your plan . . . sorry, I mean Cerberus' plan.'

'Lord Sloane is the man you should be looking–'

'With Sean lying dead in the train station in Budapest along with Magdalena and Tóth, having used them as bait, the real assassins would disappear. Within a few days, with the political demise of Churchill in the headlines of the International Press, other rumours would gain currency.'

'Did you know that Lord Slo–'

'A dead foreigner with false papers, but known as the Englander, shoots a defenceless blind woman and her little boy. Eastern Europe is a tinder-box, and everyone is waiting for the spark; even if Sean's death was not it, it would have polarised public opinion across Eastern Europe.'

The lieutenant leaned forward. 'Look, Lord Slo–'

Lenka pointed the silencer at her face. 'No one would bother with the details; it would be an international scandal with the British seen as trying to destabilise the Slav nations. Isolationist opinion in the United States would strengthen. In Eastern Europe public disorder would break out, and the Nazis would seize the excuse to march in under the pretext of restoring order. Sean knew that his death would hardly be on a par with the assassination of Archduke Ferdinand, but an innocent woman and her son murdered in broad daylight by a man supposedly working for the British Government would create the turmoil your masters sought.'

'Despite his proclamations, Churchill is not the British Government. It would–'

'Britain would be in no position to protest, once the Nazi war-machine started moving forward again. His Majesty's Government would be seen by the rest of the world as being culpable in the matter. No nation would have any sympathy for a country that was seen to ferment war.'

Amelia said nothing, but Lenka noted that for the first time the 'goddess' was perspiring.

'I detect the scent of the bitch,' said Lenka now with her finger pressed on the trigger.

The lieutenant tried to distract the Polish woman from where the conversation was going next. 'I was told that there was another assassin at the station?'

'I wouldn't call the other man on the ground an assassin; Sean believed he was to be the fall guy if Sean hadn't arrived as the woman and her child had to die.' Lenka was too wily to be side-lined. 'We all knew we had a spy in our ranks in Berlin. The Gestapo knew who to look for and even boasted that they knew I was a Jew. I disliked you as soon as your stiletto appeared on the step as you entered the underground bar in Berlin. But it was Sean who discovered that you were the traitor.'

'When did he have this Eureka moment?' asked the lieutenant, trying to appear dispassionate.

'He first told me in the Catacombs before he came to London.'

'A delusion based on drink.'

'In Amsterdam the Nazis were lying in wait for us. But, only London and the Rogues knew of the plan to get inside the factory. Sean didn't know if it was you, or someone you were reporting to. So Sean told me to relay messages to London stating that Jocky had been shot and not to mention his torture. He swore Jake, Vodanski and Chris to secrecy too, as they had killed enough Nazis to prove their worth. In London a few days later you told Sean that you were sorry to hear that Jocky had died, but you went on to ask if he thought Jocky had told the Nazis anything before he died. The Rogues had not told you of his interrogation, London didn't know, so that only left the Nazis. He knew then that you were the traitor.'

'I was only making conversation as I knew the Scotsman was his friend. You see only what you want to see. You have no–'

'When you came to the Catacombs you spoke of Jocky's torture.'

The lieutenant's bit into the crimson film on her bottom lip.

'In London when you met him at Liverpool Street

Station, you were in full uniform. He later realised that it was you he saw who had collected Magdalena and the boy in the car from outside the restaurant in Vienna. Though you kept your back to him and had your cap pressed down over your blonde hair and a different-coloured uniform, he knew it was you. Men may not notice what we wear, but they have an eye for curves. Perhaps you couldn't resist the opportunity to have a look at the man who killed so many of your colleagues in Budapest, and in whom Churchill now put his faith. Sean said that when he first met Churchill, he reminded him that "Curiosity killed the cat".' Lenka leant forward. 'Sean couldn't prove it, but he believed you slipped Magdalena something that caused them to miss the train.'

Amelia said nothing but continued to look firmly at the Polish woman.

'If all this is true, why didn't any of you kill me in the Catacombs?'

'We decided to take control of your operation in the knowledge that you had Berlin's ear. We knew that traps were being set, but we couldn't do anything about that as the bait was those we were trying to help. But after Berlin, we acted in advance of any schedule dictated by London. Sean knew you underestimated him; he enjoyed the fact that you did. Personally, Jake and I wanted to shoot you; Vodanski wanted to break your neck.'

Amelia narrowed her eyes and tried a different tactic: jealousy.

'You know that while Sean left you dying in Paris, he made love to me.'

There was not the slightest hesitation in Lenka's reply.

'No, he fucked you; he didn't make love to you. In

Paris, Sean told me that he needed evidence that you were the traitor and to unearth who else was in your network. To secure that he needed access to your house. Perhaps, at that moment, you thought that even the stupid Irishman might have been suspicious of you by now. Hence, the staged attack on both of you in London. I'm sure to protect your cover, you agreed to receive a flesh wound.' Unconsciously, Amelia lifted her hand to her neck. 'Having done so, your British superiors would believe that you were beyond reproach, perhaps promote you and give you a medal, but all it did was confirm to Sean that you were the spy.'

'Why?' asked the lieutenant, her voice starting to tremble.

'Sean confessed that when he saw you were wounded during the car chase through London, he thought he might have been wrong about you. Then he saw that you had put on an official Navy shirt that morning. You couldn't bear to ruin one of your beautiful hand-made blouses when you inflicted a flesh wound on yourself inside the car. Later, when you were shot as you lay on the road in London, it only provided further confirmation that you were the spy.'

'That makes no sense; the second bullet could have killed me!'

Lenka smiled at the outburst. 'The Alpha Wolves were the elite picked from the ranks of the SS and Gestapo. At point blank range, the man would have killed you unless he missed on purpose.'

'Then the finger should point at Sean, for he was held at gunpoint at point blank range and he wasn't even shot.'

'When Sean tracked down the gunman, Penhaligon, he weaved a tale about being interrupted by the British Secret

Service. Sean said it was a lie. Earlier in the hospital he was interviewed by his so-called saviours. He said, "They couldn't grab their arse with both hands, let alone frighten off an experienced assassin". It was all part of Cerberus' plan to let Sean escape.'

'But you said that the plan was to kill Sean?'

'Originally, but so much had happened since Budapest that the Nazis needed a credible witness to your shooting to allay any suspicions, now or in the future, that you were not a loyal subject of the King.'

'Drink has–'

'Your master needed Sean alive. After the attacks on Jake in New York, we knew that all the Rogues were a target. As I was incapacitated, Sean was the only link to finding the other Rogues. You expected that he would seek out Chris, Jake and Vodanski and bring them to me in Paris.'

'If this is true, then why were you not ambushed when you gathered in the Catacombs?'

'As Sean and I witnessed in Paris, Cerberus would not allow any Alpha Wolf squad to be led by anyone who would use their initiative. Only once we were all together could the trap finally be slammed shut. That is why Sean asked Chris to stay away from the Catacombs. As I say, Sean was now manipulating you and Cerberus.'

'Even if this is true, what has any of this got to do with me, I–'

'In Berlin, as soon as you left the Gestapo arrived and again after your visit to the Catacombs.'

'My job was to deliver information and leave. That does not make me a traitor.'

'In Amsterdam, when the Rogues were once again altogether, the Alpha Wolves were waiting for us. The next time was when they emerged from the hospital on Lake Como; you knew where I was so at last you had us all in your sights, so again the Alpha Wolves set on us. No German helicopter squadron could have scrambled so quickly that it could reach the hospital in ten minutes. You laid traps for us across Europe. But each time Sean changed the plans and with Vodanski, Jake, Chris and myself we were able to leap out of the traps, taking those you used as bait, before they were sprung.'

'But your deathly appearance when I came to the Catacombs to deliver the messages from London–'

'You mean from Berlin,' interjected Lenka, as she raised the Welrod up from the lieutenant's chest to her face.

The lieutenant swallowed hard and grasped her hands tightly on her lap. 'So, the Catacombs was all an act?'

'A little lime from the walls on my skin, and positioning the candles at a distance but above me cast shadows that exaggerated the circles under my eyes. I learnt as a child that it is easier to fool someone when you present them what they want to see.'

The lieutenant clenched her chin in defiance but the hands on her knees began to shake.

Lenka folded her finger around the trigger. 'In the Catacombs your anger was certainly not an act. Not because you believed your claim that I had betrayed you – because you were the spy – but because I exist. You must have believed that if the Jew whore didn't exist, then your bosses in Berlin would not have had to disfigure you to strengthen your cover.' Lenka smiled. 'Tell me, did you know that having given yourself a flesh wound in the car that they were going to put a bullet in that beautiful porcelain neck of yours?'

The British officer said nothing but now clenched her hands together on her lap.

Lenka could tell that the wound that had been delivered by Penhaligon had indeed been a surprise to the lieutenant. 'Finally, the train transporting the families to the Fortress was used to catch us all in Cerberus' net. Machine guns, Panzer tanks and two trains loaded with Alpha Wolves; Cerberus wanted no mistakes this time. Berlin, Amsterdam, Paris and London; we must have really pissed him and his superiors off to throw everything they had at us.'

'If you knew it was a trap that you could not possibly escape from, why walk into it for the sake of some worthless families you didn't even know?'

Lenka looked at the woman and smiled. 'That is why we are so different. It is not our religion, nor our background.'

Amelia exploded, 'You're a Jew. That is what makes us different. Your efforts will make no difference to what will happen across Europe. Now your Jew-loving friends are all dead. All that remains is a crippled Jewish whore. Even if you kill me, you will be hanged. You have no evidence of my involvement in any of what you say, and who is going to take the word of you against that of a British woman of good breeding; a member of His Majesty's naval services. Even if you are not hanged, when the Nazis seize England you will be delivered into the hands of the Gestapo for crimes against the Third Reich.'

Lenka handed a folder over to the woman. 'Open it.'

Lieutenant Brett refused but as Lenka cocked the weapon, she nervously pulled a letter from the folder. Her face froze, but her hands shook uncontrollably.

Lenka pressed the switch on Jocky's cane. The entire length of its barrel rotated, unsheathing the rapier contained in its core. Lenka thrust it into the centre of the sheet of paper. She held the traitor's gaze, as she lifted herself up as she pushed the sword gradually deeper into the British officer's heart. The paper was dripping with blood, but it had a name that was still clearly discernible. It was the name of a female British officer who had been awarded the *Kriegsverdienstkreuz* – the recently created German War Merit Cross.

As Lenka placed the empty Welrod inside her jacket, Amelia looked down transfixed by the blood spreading out across her white silk blouse.

'It takes tempered steel to fracture a block of ice,' added Lenka, as she slowly pushed the thin steel foil deeper into the stunned woman until the blood-coated blade emerged nearly a foot out the other side.

Chapter 22: Keep our Secret Safe

3 September 1939, London

Lenka stepped out into Berkeley Square. It was dawn, but a surreal red haze was already enveloping an unsuspecting London. It reminded her of the orphanage when the staff ushered the children towards the river as the red skies on the horizon heralded an uncontrollable fire approaching. All was quiet as the square was empty. Everyone it seemed was still asleep as if a spell had been cast.

If the people of England were under a spell, it was that the Nazis could be trusted. It was cast nearly a year earlier when Prime Minister Neville Chamberlain waved a piece of paper in the air, as he proudly declared, 'Peace *for* our time.'

It was clear from his speeches reported in the press that Churchill did not believe a word of it and neither did she. Sadly they were proved right. Three days earlier, German tanks had rolled into her country and reports were that soon it would fall.

With the aid of Jocky's cane, she made her way slowly down the cobbled street.

As she passed an alley on her way towards Piccadilly, she heard the cries of a child. Looking into the dark side street she thought of the last time she saw Jewel alive.

She stepped into the passageway and discovered a stocky little man screaming at a young boy lying on the cobblestones. The man raised a stick above his head and was about to bring it down when Lenka seized his wrist. The man turned and swung a haymaker of a punch at her. Lenka stepped aside from her attacker, but tripped him with the cane so he toppled, spun and landed on his back. She pushed the release button on the cane and pressed its bloody point into the dazed man's pelvis. Lenka turned to the boy.

'Who is he?'

'My mummy's new boyfriend, Ma'am.'

'Ma'am,' she smiled now thinking of Chris.

'You little bitch, I'll fu–' shouted the man, before she jabbed the blade an inch deeper releasing further screams and profanities from the man.

'Has he hit you before?' she asked, turning to the boy.

He turned his pale face to show her the broken skin and bruises under his left eye. 'Yes, and my mummy.'

Lenka pushed the point of the blade a little further into the man's pelvis. He screamed as he grabbed at the blade, slicing his fingers.

'Now you have cause to cry like a baby,' she said, as the circle of red expanded across the crotch of his trousers. 'Never go near their house, the mother or the boy again, or I will return this blade here,' stabbing it deeper, 'and slash it violently from side to side.'

The man screamed again, but nodded. Lenka withdrew the blade from his bloodied groin, letting the man curl up tightly in a ball as he attempted to muffle his sobbing.

She picked a pair of child's spectacles off the ground, rubbed the lenses on her arm and handed them to the boy. 'Yours?'

'Yes', said the boy, who couldn't take his eyes off the coiled-up body of the man. 'Is he dead?'

'He will be if he hits you again. Now, go home to your mother.'

'But he will come back when he knows you've gone.'

'You might be right,' said Lenka, who replaced the tip of the blade on the man's wound. The man was now whimpering. 'To be safe, maybe I'll cut his bollocks off,' and with that the man scrambled to his feet and scurried off. He fell twice before he disappeared into the street.

Lenka found a little café on Green Park leading up to Piccadilly Circus. Before entering she walked over to the Ritz Hotel opposite and made a telephone call from the booth next to the lobby.

On the other end of the line she was greeted by the receptionist at the Dorchester Hotel, which was only a twenty-minute walk away.

'Yes, Miss Haberman, there is a message for you,' said the genial man. 'It reads, "Miss Haberman. I will be in the hotel reception with the four children you brought from Italy at midday today."' The receptionist continued to read the note verbatim. '"My master," Si Bengareine, "gave me instructions to buy them warm clothes as he has heard that Ireland experiences bitter winters. Your faithful servant, Ahmed."'

The receptionist added that the young man wrote the message himself as sadly I believe he was unable to speak.

'Thank you. Please tell Ahmed that I will be there at noon,' she said before she placed the phone on the receiver. The Rector had delivered on his promise to Sean and had kept the children from the facility on Lake Como safe within the walls of the Paris Mosque.

Lenka hobbled across the deserted main thoroughfare towards the café. The boat train, which connected with the ferries to Ireland, did not leave from Euston Station for Holyhead for another eight hours. There is plenty of time, she said to herself.

Sean had told her that his sister Marisa was raising a number of waifs and strays in a big house just outside Cork. When Lenka arrived in Paris with the families liberated from Cerberus' train she sent a telegram to Marisa. Sean's sister replied two days later saying she would welcome her offer to help, particularly as she had, unlike herself, considerable experience of running an orphanage. Lenka quickly sent another message to ask if there was room for any more children. This included Selena and Gretchen whose foster home in Hampstead turned out to be only a temporary arrangement. Marisa replied, 'Bring as many as you can. I'll sleep on the floor if needs be.' Lenka smiled when she read this as Marisa sounded so much like her brother.

Lenka placed her hand on the envelope inside her jacket. It contained the banker's draft that still had Chris' bloodied fingerprints on it. Katherine and Chris' legacy meant that Marisa's home would be able to feed many more children as the war spread across Europe.

She placed the tip of her cane on the stone step and entered the café. Behind the bar the manager was restocking the shelves before his first customer of the day arrived. He was too late. 'Brandy,' called Lenka.

'Morning madam. It's a bit early for–' but when he was

met by the woman's steely eyes he turned to the bottles behind him.

'Any particular type madam?'

'A double,' she shouted over her shoulder, as she took a seat at the table at the farthest end of the restaurant.

The owner was tuning the radio in to the BBC as the prime minister was to make an announcement at 11:15 that morning. She knew what the announcement on the radio would be. The Nazis had been issued an ultimatum by Britain and France to agree to withdraw from Poland by 11:00 – of course it would be ignored. The British prime minster would have to tell the nation it would soon be at war. Lenka rested the cane against the table. For the first time she noticed the very small lettering etched into the handle. She smiled as she read the message, no doubt made by its maker:

Be a Lover Not a Fighter. J x

She looked at the child's white knitted hat in her hand. Two days ago on the ferry to England, she had thought of leaving it unwashed as the child's hat was the only memento she had of Dominique and two of the fiercest fighters she had ever known. Having washed it a number of times since her arrival in London, the blood stains were gone, but she smiled, knowing that the men would not mind if it was used as it was originally intended. Instinctively she lifted it up to her nose as if to catch a scent of the Rogues – not surprisingly there was none.

She wiped away a tear, the first since she was a child.

Perhaps it was for her country that could not

withstand the superior firepower of the Wehrmacht for long. Maybe it was for Leo, for Olen, for Jewel. She gently held the little hat to her eyes; so many had died.

She remembered after Jewel's death saying to Jake, 'It is always the innocent who are the first to die.' He replied, 'Then we shall walk this Earth for eternity.' He was wrong – Jake along with Vodanski, Jewel, Chris, Jocky and Sean were all dead too. Lenka watched the bar manager as he turned up the volume of the radio behind the bar before he walked over to her table with the large brandy on a silver tray.

'Is no one joining you madam?' asked the manager.

'It's just me for now,' replied the Polish woman, as she placed her hand on her stomach. She sat quietly and thought of the future, and wondered if her child's eyes would change to glacial-blue whenever it felt threatened.

Also by the same author

The Benevolence of Rogues

Aid worker's missions find unlikely support from prison forgers, gangster's henchmen and sympathetic police... John Righten has been in the wrong place at the right time since the 1980s. Then, he was in Romania, delivering medical supplies to orphans suffering from Aids. Subsequently he was in Bosnia in the 90s, sneaking in medical supplies and in South America – Brazil, Chile and Peru – during the 2000s. Righten is now back and has put together his experiences in his autobiography, The Benevolence of Rogues.

Hampstead & Highgate Express (UK)

This is not a memoir for the straight-laced, politically correct or faint of heart: massive quantities of alcohol are consumed, many teeth are knocked out and sarcasm is in generous supply.

Kirkus Independent (US)

Also, available on Amazon are the first and second novels in the Rogues Trilogy:

Churchill's Rogue

&

The Gathering Storm

The Bookbag review Churchill's Rogue (UK & US)

Sean Ryan grew up in Ireland during the 20th century's first quarter and so understands death and loss. He learnt to defend what he felt right during his time as a bodyguard for Michael Collins. Therefore when Winston Churchill called upon his services in 1937 to bring a mother and child out of Germany, Ryan doesn't say no. However Ryan soon discovers this is no easy escort duty. The mother and child in question are for some reason being hunted by an elite German force led by Cerberus, a code name for a sadist incarnate. On the plus side, Ryan soon discovers he's not alone. There are more like him across Europe; those with pasts that forged them into violent defenders of the vulnerable in an increasingly dangerous world. These are the Rogues and, this time, Ryan needs their help.

This is British author John Righten's debut novel following the first instalment of his non-fiction autobiography Benevolence of Rogues which brought to the fore some of the real life 'Rogues' he's met during a multi-faceted life spent in some very dangerous places. John isn't someone who has just had an exciting, precariously balanced life; he also has a talent for transferring such existences to the page. Anyone doubting this should certainly read Churchill's Rogues – and hold onto your seats!

To be fair, the novel has a bit of a false start. At the beginning the scene is set as Churchill meets Ryan in the former's office to discuss the Irishman's mission. This is a scene that's nothing like the rest of the story. In this short opener the discussion feels a little stilted in places and historical fact feels as though it's been shoe-horned in. However this is a passing moment compared to the rest of the novel, so short it doesn't affect the perfect rating and so passing that it's soon forgotten in a flurry of tense, bloody brilliance.

Once Ryan leaves Churchill the historical facts are added in a more subtle way, providing fascinating insight into a Germany in which Hitler has swept himself to power and the atrocities in the name of 'racial cleansing' are being introduced with increasing intensity. Churchill's involvement is interesting as, in an era when the UK and US were dithering as to whether the Nazis should be fought or be expeditiously befriended, the future Prime Minister was a lone voice of almost prophetic warning.

Although there are other factual characters appearing (e.g. Himmler and the Fuhrer himself) the most compelling are the fictionalised. Sean Ryan is almost a 1930s Irish Jack Reacher and yet, as much as I love Lee Child's work (and I do love it!), John Righten adds rugged, scream-curdling realism and a pace that would render Jack Reacher an asthmatic wreck.

Speaking of scream-curdling brings us to the most wonderful baddie in the Earl Grey drinking Cerberus. His real name – Major Krak - may give rise to a smirk or two but we don't laugh for long. He enjoys torture and, to give him credit, he's certainly got an imagination for it.

Indeed, earlier I described the novel as 'bloody' and for a good reason; it's definitely not a story for the delicate. However, the intensity of violence isn't for gratification. It reminds us that in the real world shootings and explosions don't just produce a tidy red dot on victims' bodies; death can be a messy business!

The other thing we notice is that this is doesn't suffer from that usual first in series malady, set-up-lull. As we follow the pasts and presents of Australian, Russian, American and British Rogues we back-track them through other conflicts like the Spanish Civil War and the Russian Revolution. The more we come to know them, the more we can't help loving them while also realising why it's best not to get close to anyone in this line of work. We're at the mercy of an author who will kill at will (in literary terms) but having started on the emotional roller coaster, I don't want to the series to end. Bring on The Gathering Storm – I'm braced and more than ready!

Printed in Great Britain
by Amazon.co.uk, Ltd.,
Marston Gate.